DA $TREETS RAISED ME & DA GUNS PAID ME

A Thugs' Journey

Juvi & Splash Queen

Da $treets Raised Me
& Da Guns Paid Me

Printed in the United States of America.

ISBN: 978-1-7366158-1-2

Table of Contents

Bonus Book

Chapter One

The streets was below zero minus the wind chill. It was December 28, 2018, one year after infamous Joaquin "Shorty" Guzman—El Chapo—escaped from a housed Mexican maximum security facility. Since El Chapo's arrest, dope prices increased like gas prices. Once where 17.5 was standard price, it now became twenty-five flat a key. A lot of shady business was being conducted. The brick man was water whipping and distributing slabs, then sending the thirsty wolves to strip the purchaser. While a dirty game was on, there was a handful of real street niggas that played as well. They weren't affected by the prolonged drought. Thug was one of them. Thug was on a mission to get the green by any means necessary. Thug crotched down below Gunplay's windowsill. Gunplay was the man you went to see when you was hungry. He always had chicken dinners for the low like Shawty Lo. That made him a susceptible prime target for robbery.

Condensation appeared on the outside of the window as Thug peered into Gunplay's bedroom. Thug was bundled tightly in a Carhart coat, black Saint Laurent jeans, black ACGs, with a ski-mask pulled low over his face. His .9mm was equipped with a 30 round stick which he slipped in the confines of his coat pocket. He gently eased the frosted, partially cracked window open and climbed into the dark room. Considering the dilapidated facade, Thug was astounded to find the interior of Gunplay's residence immaculate.

Thug flipped the mattress over and got to work. Bundles of money and cocaine lined the mattress. The merch was in the exact spot the lil thot Diamond had informed him it would be. Diamond was a dime who made all the dope boys fall in love. When she got them in her clutches, she made lovesick niggas feel like they was only one that they'd grocery bagged. The truth of the matter was… money made her cum. Money talked and bullshit walked. Because Gunplay didn't live by such motto, he was about to lose a fortune. Gunplay showed Diamond in confidence, in a fit of passion, where he kept the stash. *How dumb could niggas be*, Thug thought.

Thug stripped the pillowcase of the bedding and proceeded to fill it with merch. In the process of stuffing the content, Thug heard movement coming from elsewhere in the house. He froze and gripped his gun. He could have sworn he heard the floorboards creak. But after a while of silence, Thug resumed his task. Tying the sack, he tossed the merchandise out the window into the snow. As he climbed on the dresser to exit, a lamp fell and shattered on the floor.

"Shit!" Thug cussed under his breath. Not giving his clumsiness a second thought, he moved to get out the window. The bedroom door crashed open followed by a chain of gunfire that erupted from Gunplay's Mac-11. A bullet struck Thug in the bicep, causing him to tumble out the window face first. In a panic, he struggled to scramble to his feet. Thug's pant leg was caught on a rusty nail. Snagging with all his might, he unhitched himself, ripping his jeans in the process. Thug withdrew his face popper and leaned up against the house. The rapid gunfire purged, and silence spread through the night. Only Thug's heavy breathing and Gunplay's footsteps rushing toward the window could be heard. Thug leveled his gun, preparing himself for the kill. Gunplay stuck his head into the night, and Thug placed the muzzle to his chin. He fired three times, turning his head into a bowling ball. Gunplay's blood was splattered everywhere. His body hung halfway out the window, and his blood mingled in the snow like a slushy.

Thug stood up and sent another slug through Gunplay. He then picked up the pillowcases and fled into the night leaving droplets of blood along the trail. As he hopped in his forest green 84 T-top Cutless and smashed the gas, he thought, *this is the end result for niggaz who thought with their dicks and pillow talked to hoes.*

Thug sped through the night dialing a friend's number in his Galaxy Note 9.

"Hello" Faye answered.

"Come open da door" Thug demanded hoarsely, hanging up.

Minutes later his Lowpro came to halt in front of Faye's tip. Halfway on the curb, Thug dashed through the cold and pounded on her front door loud enough to wake the neighbors.

"Damn, nigga, why you knockin' on my door like you ain't got no damn sense?". Faye said in frustration swinging open the door. "You just called. What, you thought I'd leave yo ass out there in da cold?"

"I've been hit" Thug pushed past her, rushing to the sofa and flopped down.

"What you talkin' bout?" Faye was puzzled.

Thug removed his coat. "I've been shot..." he said, showing her his wounded arm.

"Boy, what the fuck...!" she exclaimed in horror, taking Thug by his arm.

Faye wasn't your average hood chick. She was a CNA by night attending Marquette university by day to study business. At 22, she wanted something out of life. To move on up like the Jefferson's.

"What you then got yourself into now? You always out there on them streets wildin' out. You do know this ain't da wild-wild west, right?"

This wasn't the first time she had to nurse Thug back to health. A couple months back, he'd been involved in some other cowboy action. Shooting it out in the streets with some sneak dissing clown that was bad mouthing him on the internet. When they crossed paths, Thug let them hammers talk. Amidst the blaze of glory, Thug took one to the leg. Faye couldn't remove the 40-caliber bullet. He was at risk of infection. Gangrene could set in and could result in death. Thug didn't fear or care. He took it like a gangsta. It was just another war wound dedicated to thug life. He was back for a second time within months. Wounded from another gun fight, Thug could never risk the hospital. Faye's comfort and aid would do. It saved him from the police meddling in his mix with tedious interrogations and possible investigations. Faye was a dear friend Thug knew he could confide in and they'd been as tight as spandex fitting an elephant since he was thirteen and she eighteen.

Thug was a hoodlum who was always making noise in the hood. Faye was a timid, quiet type of girl when they met. It wasn't by chance that they met. Faye was a goddess that stood 5'2", weighing in at 130 pounds. Curves and measurements 32-24-36 that was complimented by her dark silky hair, light brown eyes. In his state of mind, Thug approached Faye on the block and shot his shot. He was declined due to the age difference, but that still didn't hinder a friendship from flourishing.

"Boy, your ass just gonna keep on playin' with fiya until you get burned, huh?" she retorted with concern.

"I'm already burnin'. I was born in hell. So gone with all that Mutha Theresa shit. It's gonna take more than a flesh wound to put me down for the count. Gangstas don't die, we multiply."

* * * * *

Keys and her right-hand man, Demon, pulled up in their hood on 38th & Garfield. In her candy blueberry 2018

Lincoln Navigator L Black Label, sitting on 30-inch matching Forgis. They parked behind her brother Cam'ron's grape jam color 2019 Infiniti Qx50. He paid a pretty penny to cop it before it even came out. They was living large, they lived like bosses.

"Imma keep it real with ya, Keys" Demon said in between puffs of the finest Gorilla glue you could find on the street market. "I don't think it's wise to let Candy handle that bizness transaction with Krazy and his crew. You should let me deal with that lil bizness" he said.

"I appreciate your offer, but you know wat I do is always for da team's best interest" Keys replied. "My daughter Candy and her coed friend are the only ones who can fly the coupe under the radar" she said.

"I respect that. Imma ride with ya, whatever decision you make. I just want you to keep in mind them niggas cut" he told her.

Keys took heed to what Demon was saying. Demon was her go-to man whenever she needed something. They was thick as thieves. She knew Demon was only looking out for her.

"I know what ya mean" Keys assured. "But this is how it has to be" she went on. Keys only relied upon her daughter indulging within family business when she felt there was no alternative solution. Candy was a last resort card she played every blue moon. Plus, Keys wasn't too concerned about the situation at hand. Candy had done business with Krazy and his shadow, Bagz, before. For a measly half of slab, but this was 25 kilos, a considerable amount of merch. Keys understood why Demon was on edge. Keys hands was tied. She couldn't put Demon behind the wheel with that astronomical amount of flake. It wasn't that she didn't trust him, they fucked with each other the long way. Demon just didn't fit the bill to evade twelve. Everything about Demon spelled hoodfigga. He was a six foot muscle bound killer covered in tattoos from head to toe. The facial tats alone made the boyz in blue suspicious. He was prone to profiling. The vehicle would be searched. If Candy was pulled over, the officer was more likely be mesmerized by her big butt and smile. Candy had been blessed with her looks. She was a spitting image of Keys. They both was high yellow, long jet-black hair, hazel eyes and with full juicy lips. Their bodies was a work of art. Standing 5'6" and a 125 pounds with an ass that made niggas double take and get whiplash passing by. They looked like twins, matching in every asset.

"Plus, Candy can handle her own" Keys said confidently. "She's insidious. She play more harmless than she really is. My blood pumps in her veins, so she got da heart of a lioness. Just send a hit squad to make sure everythang ran smoothly."

"Fa'sha, Imma get on that" Demon said and passed Keys the weed.

"Matta fact, let me hit her ass up right now and have her link up with us over here." Keys said, dialing Candy's number.

"What up, ma?" Candy answered on the first ring.

"You know, out here clockin' dolla signs" Keys replied. "You still in ten toes on that B.I. right?"

"Ma, you know I stand on my word. I don't do no backin' out. I'm ready when you ready" she said.

"Alright, that's what I like to hear" Keys inhaled the bud into her lungs. "Pull up on me at da trap so we can go over da playbook" she instructed.

"Alright, give me a minute though. I'm finna go swoop my gurl, Ecstasy, and Imma be there in about half an hour" she replied.

Ecstasy was Candy's partner in crime. They were always together. Candy never went anywhere without her. Ecstasy was what you would refer to as a gutta chick. She got down for the cause and always had Candy's back. Although they differed in the look department, Ecstasy was still a bad bitch. She had almond skin, dark eyes, and a Rihanna hair style. Her beauty compared with that of her 36-28-36 measurements.

"I'll be waitin'" Keys concluded then hung up the phone. "Let's roll up in here and see what lil bro ass on." she said hopping out of the truck.

* * * * *

Detective Benson and his partner Brown were the first homicide detectives to arrive at the scene after the first responders. The paramedics tried their best to revive the stiff, but the victim had already been dead on arrival for approximately nine hours. The blood had already started to coagulate. Benson had been a homicide detective for a decade. Before then, he'd been a regular decorated officer for five years patrolling the North side of Milwaukee, during which time he had witnessed many murders. A corpse laid in the snow. Droplets of blood were found down the bottleneck walkway to the alley, then disappeared. Forensics was photographing the scene. The medical examiner was upon the scene too. Benson waited for the coroner to do their part and remove the body for further analysis so the cause of death could be determined. The cause was evident to Benson and Brown. A bullet to the head resulted in the victim's death, but a pathologist had to perform an autopsy to determine the exact cause of death.

"Karma is a bitch, isn't it?" Brown whispered to Benson apathetically.

"Yeah, I know what you mean" Benson replied

They were both familiar with the deceased. Gunplay Gucci Jackson had been a pain in their asses for quite some time. Just the year before, he'd been suspected of a triple homicide that fatally claimed two and left one injured. There was too many loose ends to successfully tie Gunplay to the crime. A CI gave them enough information to make an arrest. While Gunplay was in custody, the CI was gunned down.

"It was only a matter of time" Brown offered.

"Ain't that the truth..." Benson agreed.

Gunplay had been like a gunslinger for years throughout Milwaukee. Now his choice of lifestyle had come back to bite him on the ass.

"What direction do we start with this matter at hand?" Brown asked. They had no suspects in custody and no information that pointed them to the one responsible. That bothered Brown a smidgen. He wanted the scum responsible off the street as soon as possible before he had a chance to kill again. Benson chuckled.

"We don't start anywhere. He deserved what he got" Benson answered coldly. "After this mess is cleaned up, we let the streets do our job. Everybody knows somebody that know somebody that know something. So, we let the dead bury the dead" Benson said, like it meant nothing. It was clear to him most of law enforcement's job was based on information provided to them. Utilizing street resources, cops normally solved the crime within 48 hours. The new generations didn't stick to the code the old heads had put in play. There was no more snitches get stitches. Everyone was out for themselves. Benson knew it was only a matter of time before someone opened their mouth with the information that would lead them to the one responsible.

* * * * *

Meek Mills' new song "Triumph" chimed through Thug's cellphone.

"S'up" Thug answered without glancing at the display.

"Wuz poppin', my nigga?" Snake asked.

Snake was Thug's homie. Cut from the same cloth and breed. Most would call him a cold-blooded reptile; but to the team he was loyal. It was to outsiders that he struck out and bit.

"You alright, how that muv go last night?"

"Like takin' candy from a baby" Thug replied. "I'm good on this end. I took a bullet in da process, but Imma soulja. So, you know I'm still strong after da obstacle course" he said.

"W-what..." Snake stuttered in concern. "What 'cha mean you took a bullet?"

"Just what I said. Bitch ass nigga popped me as I was fleein' with da money bag" Thug responded.

"You see, nigga, I told yo ass you should've took me or that nigga Trouble with cha" Snake scolded.

Trouble was their ace boon. His name spoke for itself. He could go from zero to a hundred real quick. Most called him the Grim Reaper. When his guns went bang, he was the last person you saw.

"That solo dolo shit ain't what up. You got hitters on da team, use them."

"My nigga, what are you, my dad?" Thug joked. "What's understood, needs not to be discussed. You don't need to sell yourself to me. I know you and fam get down" Thug stressed, stretching his wounded arm. The muscle had begun to stiffen and cause discomfort.

"Look, I ain't about to keep it rappin' on this line. Come swoop me up" Thug said.

"Where you at?" Snake asked.

Snake was already in traffic scheming on his next lit. The concept of the early bird gets the worm stuck with him. So, when the sun came up, he was out in search of his next bag.

"I'm at Faye's crib" Thug told him.

"Ah, your boo thang." Snake teased. "Soft ass nigga, soon as you get shot, you wanna go runnin' over there so she can kiss your boo-boo all betta" he joked.

"Fool stop, you know it ain't that type of party. Me and Faye jus be chillin'. Get' cha mind out da gutta" Thug replied.

"Nigga please, who you think you foolin'? Save that platonic bullshit to Plato. You and I both know if da opportunity arise, you cram that" Snake said.

They both laughed. Thug had to respect the real bro. Because he knew his boy was keeping it one hundred.

"Man fuck all that, come get me fool" Thug said.

"I'm on my way" Snake reassured him.

Moments later Snake was honking his horn. The bass from his slappers in the trunk shook the ground.

Thug grabbed his blood-stained coat and headed for the front door. He grabbed the pillowcase from the trunk of his ride and satchel, then jumped in Snake's black and gold 87 box Chevy Caprice sitting on 28 DUBs.

"My nigga, what's good?" Snake greeted, flashing his mouth full of 18 carat gold teeth. Snake was a tall, dark nigga that looked like Gucci Mane. So, when he smiled, all you could see was his teeth.

"You know, livin' like a boss" Thug said, sparking up a blunt of Exotic that he'd pearled early in the morning while collecting his thoughts.

"Would thta be da reason you think you got a personal chauffeur too?" Snake asked turning down the sounds. "Call me to come pick you up when you got your own hot wheels…"

"Fool ass nigga, I called you to come get me because I didn't wanna drive under da influence. Faye gave me some of them Perc 30s she had layin' around. Nigga feel like he walkin' on water" Thug explained exhaling a cloud of smoke. "Let's hit tha trap and see what that nigga Trouble up to" he said.

"Fa' sho." Snake agreed smashing the gas.

Sounds of flesh slapping and female moans were heard from the corner bedroom. Thug and Snake noticed as soon as they entered the trap house. The kitchen table was a mess. A high beam scale sat on the table, rocked up dope, and razor blade occupied a saucer on the counter, plus corner cut baggies were scattered about the floor and table.

"Look at this nigga" Thug complained about the condition of the spot. "This nigga in here thinkin' with his dick, with all this shit lyin' around. Ain't nobody in here to watch over him or nothin'. At least he could've had one of da other homies on da spot with em. Fam help me clean this shit up" Thug said, looking around.

"I gotcha" Snake replied, helping Thug clean up. "You know you can't even sweat this shit though. It's to be expected from that nigga. You and I both know that nigga and he ain't gone change. He been like this forever" Snake continued. Trouble was careless and reckless. He didn't have a care in the world.

"You ain't gotta tell me. I know what's good" Thug confirmed. "I just want that nigga to tighten ' up. He can't keep bein' loose. Discipline is key. We tryna reach da big league. A lot of people get brought down at da top from someone on da inside with sloppiness. Without discipline, there is no structure" he went on.

"Already, my nigga" Snake agreed.

Snake was well aware how one should conduct themselves. Always in orderly fashion. Snake bled the streets. He'd been on the streets since he was nine. His mother and father were killed in a horrible car crash by a drunk driver driving down the wrong side of the highway. From then on, he'd been forced by court order to live with his auntie. The living conditions was horrible. Drugs played a major factor. His auntie Tina Rose was strung out something bad. So, all the checks the state provided for his care always ended up lining the pockets of the dope man, which left Snake with no positive role model or suitable future. That left Snake with two choices, the streets or die.

"You know I know what it do. Just another day of da life" Snake said.

"Now we just gotta make that nigga see da vision" Thug said setting the pillowcase and satchel on the chair. "This trap is our dinner plate and we have to keep it clean if we want to eat another meal off of it, feel me?" he asked rhetorically.

The sounds of lovemaking ceased in the bedroom, and Trouble came out sweaty in nothing but a pair of jeans.

"Wuz crackin' my nigga?" Trouble enthused embracing both Snake and Thug.

"Watch da arm..." Thug warned easing Trouble back. "This muthafucka hurt, so be easy" he said.

"What's up with da cast anyways?" Trouble inquired.

"Nigga had to strip somethin' last night, and I got popped" Thug answered.

"I hope you sent that nigga to da upper room" he said. Trouble had put in so much work, that now he enjoyed hearing other niggas' war stories.

"That's a nigga pass to heaven" he said.

"You know I trumped that boy" Thug confirmed, giving the homies dap. There was a sense of pride in his tone. "Three shots and one" he explained.

"That's what I'm talkin' bout." Trouble said. "What's in da bag, though?"

"A gift for da family" Thug added, rubbing his hands like an evil scientist. "As soon as you get rid of company. I'll unwrap it" he said.

"Shit…" Trouble slurred. "Wifey bout to leave in a minute. Jackie gettin' dressed right now" he continued.

Jackie came out the room where she and Trouble had just copulated. Her hair was disheveled. Unkept hair was a sign of indiscretion. Still, she was exquisite and alluring. She looked good enough to eat, like Kerri Hilson. One look at her and there was no doubt that pretty girls rocked. She was as sweet as mead.

"I'll see you later" she kissed Trouble on the lips. "I had fun. I can't wait to see you later tonight" she told him showing her anticipation by grabbing his dick through his jeans.

"You betta slow up b' fo you don't make it to work" he told her.

"You promise?" she teased giggling like a schoolgirl. "Let me get up out of here before I be late. You better bring yo ass home tonight too" she said.

"Gotcha" he responded.

"I ain't playin' either. Don't make me come lookin' for yo ass" she joked, teasing him further.

"What you gon do, arrest me?" he joked.

They shared another passionate kiss, then Jackie jostled her Chanel purse on her shoulder and sashayed out the door.

"I don't know how your Tone Loc lookin' ass be catchin' pieces like that" Snake blurted out as soon as Jackie was out of earshot.

"All I hear is hate, hate, hate comin' from your mouth" Trouble shot back.

They all laughed. Ribbing each other was a ritual. They were all playaz and Trouble knew his boy was just jerking his chain. Women from all walks of life would consider Trouble handsome. His rich brown skin tone complemented his six-foot, 235-pound mesomorph body covered in tattoos.

"If you must know, I hit her with da philter" Trouble said.

"With da filter?" Snake questioned confused. "We knew you was dirty, but I didn't know you was hittin' bitches with porous devices.

"Fool, not that kind" Trouble laughed at his boy's ignorance. "P.H.I.L.T.E.R.." He spelled out. "That luv potion with yo crazy ass."

"Alright, that's enough foolin' around" Thug intervened, still cracking up. "Real talk, I'm glad you got shawty in your corner. But money over bitches, so, let's focus on this bread" he said.

They counted the money and weighed up the dope. It totaled out to fifty-five grand and a whole thang.

"It ain't much my niggaz, but we climbin' up da corporate ladder together" Thug announced. "Let's make a pact as Pringle gang. Together we stand, divided we fall" he summoned, sticking out his hand. Snake and Trouble both placed their hands over one another and repeated the pact. PG was a family. United they stand, divided they fall.

Chapter Two

* * * * *

C andy and Ecstasy were having a tete-à-tete conversation within the interior of Candy's candy apple red 2018 Alfa Romeo Giulia Q2 Ti Sport. They patiently waited for Krazy and Bagz to arrive. Candy took a quick peek at her Arpels Planetarium ladies watch, the time was 9:15 pm. Krazy was already late. The Cracker Barrel off I-94 parking lot was fairly deserted except for a few scattered unattended cars.

"So, what you got on da agenda after we let da birds fly south for da winter?" Ecstasy asked. Krazy was a shot caller for the two-one syndicate that dwelled on the South side of Milwaukee.

"Now that midterms over with, Imma take a bag and tear da mall down before we hit Time Square up in NYC" Candy replied with glee. "I already wanna have my swag game before I bless tha city with all this beauty." She placed her hands beneath her chin and batted her mink eyelashes while simultaneously pouting her full lips like Nikki Minaj.

"Gurl, you so conceited, it don't make no sense" Ecstasy laughed, waving her friend off. "But don't you think we should wait to tear down da store when we land?"

They were scheduled to take the red eye flight early in the morning of December 31st. They wanted to be there to experience the electrifying atmosphere when the ball dropped for New Year's.

"Imma do that too. Money come and money go. Ain't like you can take it with you. So, wherever a bitch go, Imma blow a bag."

Candy didn't have a sense for the value of money. Her family was stacked with a lot of dead presidents like the Rockefellers, so money wasn't a thing. Krazy and Bagz rolled up making the ground quake in their off-white Cadillac Escalade. Candy was relieved they decided to show, but furious with them at the same time. Their daily schedule didn't consist on waiting around in a parking lot for a nigga to arrive.

"Well, if it isn't beauty and da beast…" Krazy barbed towards Ecstasy who leaned shoulder to shoulder on Candy's luxury vehicle. His facetious demeanor didn't get a rise out of her. Only a smug smile creased her lips.

"Ha, ha, ha…" Ecstasy returned sardonically. "Real funny, Daddy Yankee lookin' muthafucka" she retorted.

Ecstasy and Krazy had history. They shared a year of passionate bliss, embraced in the contentment of mutual attraction. Their time was spent like a fairytale, and it had Ecstasy building castles in the sky, dreaming one day they'd be bonded in holy matrimony. Krazy always wined and dined her. Treated her like a queen. Unfortunately, all good things must come to an end. Things had gone sour. She caught Krazy red-handed in their bed with another woman. Ecstasy was furious and humiliated. Krazy tried, on numerous occasions, to reconcile, but she vowed never to forgive him. In the end, they parted ways, but there was tension between the two.

"I'm lyin', you still make my heart flutter" Krazy smiled, winked, and crossed his hand over his chest in a chivalrous manner.

"Eat your heart out" Ecstasy said, giving him the finger.

"Enough with all this passive-aggressive shit" Candy interrupted.

Candy was well aware of the animosity her friend held for Krazy, but she couldn't blame her.

"You already late and I got shit to do. So, chill with all da shenanigans and let's get down to bizness" Candy had her mother Keys' attitude when it came to money. Bullshit and money getting didn't mix. Plus, JLo and Ciara were both scheduled to attend the New Year's Eve bash, and Candy herself was surely looking forward to seeing the performance.

"Nice to see you too" Krazy sarcastically countered. "How you been?"

"I'm good, now where da money at?" Candy cut to the chase. "Like I said, a bitch got shit to do."

"Where da product?"

"You'll see it as soon as I see da cash. Money talk bullshit walk" she said.

Candy didn't like the back-and-forth shit, but she knew it was required with the caliber of nigga she was dealing with. Krazy was an emotional type of dude who felt he had to have the last word. It was hard to tell if he was nigga or thot. She couldn't comprehend what her friend saw in him in the first place. She knew love was blind, but not that blind. Krazy was a bitch in a nigga vessel in her eyes. "Grab da loot so we can school da college girl in da trade of da dope game" he pressed.

Candy didn't appreciate Krazy's comment. Candy knew about the dope game way before she developed a notion of being a lawyer. She was born in it but felt no need to stress her certified credentials.

"Negro, please, before I ever let an immense imbecile school me in something that breed me in bread and butter, it'll be a cold day in hell" Candy reciprocated, folding her arms while simultaneously rolling her and eyes. "Now that we got that out our system, can we get down to handlin' bizness. Time is money and I don't plan on losin' either" she snapped back at him.

Krazy felt Candy's attitude was out of pocket. There was nothing more he despised than a woman who talked out her necklace. Deep down, he was a masochist and didn't like women who tried to stand up and thought had authority over men. Candy automatically picked up on Krazy's mood swing. It was clear he felt some type of way. She didn't care. Bagz fetched the duffle bag from the back seat of their truck and placed it on Candy's hood.

"There's da cash right there. Now where da product?" Bagz asked.

"Gurl, grab that shit out da trunk, so I can get these niggaz out my face." Candy told Ecstasy. As soon as the words left her mouth, a funny vibe washed over her spine. It made her reluctant to push forward with the transaction. Candy was just ready to wash her hands with Krazy and Bagz, 'cause they were irking the hell out her last nerve. Ecstasy placed the bag on the hood also.

"Well, let me see da what 'cha workin' with..." Krazy requested. "Like you said, time is money. So, let's get this show on da road" he said.

Candy resented patronizing pompous assholes with monkey see monkey do attitudes. He thought he was being clever by mocking her.

"Please, don't even try to play me like I'm new to this" Candy clutched at her pink automatic 380 in her holster, that had CCW to carry. "I ain't new to this, I'm true to this. You know how da game go. Cash first!"

Krazy chuckled. "You a feisty one, ain't cha?" he asked unzipping the bag. He took a couple bundles out and tossed them on the hood.

Candy took initiative and thumbed through the bills. "W-what da fuck is this?" she confronted him.

The bag contained dummy knots. With blueberries on top of blank paper wrapped in a rubber band.

"Da end" Krazy growled, pulling the trigger of his .44 Desert Eagle concealed in his Louis Vuitton men's hoodie. The bullet tore a large gap in Candy's abdomen. Candy stumbled back in a daze. She was taken by surprise. In a panic, she tried to unhitch her own weapon, but it was no use. Before she could get it out, Krazy face-timed her. The bullet went right through her cheek. The next bullet blew her eye socket, splattering Ecstasy's face. Ecstasy was hysterical, cradling her best friend's head in her arms. "Nooooo!" She wailed. "C-Candy get up! You gotta wake up…" she screamed, torn apart. Ecstasy tried making sense of the vicious game. She didn't realize though the game was fair, it was cold.

"You punk ass bitch!" she screamed lunging at Krazy, but he shoved her back.

"It's betta than bein' worm feed" Krazy retorted and squeezed a single shot. The bullet struck Ecstasy in the chest, leaving her slumped against the panel of Candy's Alfa Romeo. "Let's be out" he told Bagz. They grabbed the merch and fled. Krazy and Bagz dived in their respective trucks and a fusillade off .223 slugs perforated the back window as they fishtailed off the scene.

* * * * *

Bullet rolled through the heart of the streets of Milwaukee in his Jay-Z blue 2018 F-Type Jaguar coupe blasting "From

Babies To Man" by Tee Grizzley. His Galaxy Samsung sat on his lap. He'd been trying to contact Gunplay all morning but was unsuccessful. They had business, and he was unlike Gunplay to put money on the back burner. Bullet was on his way to handle it when his phone vibrated. Checking the screen display, he quickly answered.

"What up, lil partna?" he spoke to Parlay holding the phone away from his face.

Parlay was one of the youngest Wonder Bread members. He'd earned his stripes by putting in major work.

"They got Gunplay" Parlay murmured into the receiver.

"What?" Bullet asked. He barely heard Parlay. His deep voice came through as a faint whisper.

"You gotta speak up, I can't hear you" Bullet said.

"They hit Gunplay, I said" he repeated. "He dead" he said.

"Stop playin', dawg—" Bullet scoffed in disbelief. Real niggas didn't die. "I just dropped that nigga at his tip last fuckin' night. My nigga a rider, not a coward" he lamented, thinking Gunplay was invincible.

"Look, my nig, I'm too real for games…" Parlay sighed. "I'm on da scene right now and twelve everywhere, with da block wrapped in yellow tape" he said.

"I'm on my way" Bullet replied.

Moments later, Bullet parked his whip on the corner of his boy's block. It was just as Parlay said. Police trudged the neighborhood. A throng of nosey neighbors gathered as if some spectacle was taking place. Bullet silently approached Parlay. No words exchanged between them. Parlay's head hung low, and his eyes drooped. The facial expression spoke volumes. When the EMTs wheeled Gunplay's lifeless body into the back of the wagon, Parlay exploded.

"Man, that's fucked up. On da gee somebody gon pay for this shit. As God is my witness…" he pounded his fist into his other palm. Bullet couldn't agree more with Parlay. When he found who responsible, it would be church singing and flower bringing. Bullet was a natural born killer. He claimed his first body at the tender age of sixteen. At that age he was naturally small, 5'6" and weighing 110 pounds soaking wet. Real small, but had a lot of heart. When you're young, no one ever acknowledges how perniciously vicious you can be. There was always someone trying to gain stripes off the weakest link. They were like hyenas. Confident in a pack, but cowardly lions alone.

That was Leroy Parker AKA Lex fatal mistake. Palaski Highschool let out early in the afternoon. Bullet sat on 27th Street bus stop waiting on his route. When the wannabe gangsta Lex and his minions walked up, Bullet paid them no mind. His intentions was on getting to the block to hustle his pack off. Money was on his mind. Out of nowhere Lex snatched his frames off his face.

"Let me see them joints" he snapped.

"You might wanna put em back where you found em" Bullet calmly said.

"Or what?" Lex challenged. "Since we talkin' bout what I might like to do, I might wanna go in your pockets" Lex's flunkies cackled like a bunch of hens at his remark.

Bullet didn't find the humor in the statement. Through it all, he kept his composure. What Lex didn't know was Bullet would introduce him to the element of surprise. Only when the time was right. They were a half a block from the police district. When Bullet struck, there would be no one to save Lex. "Alright, you got it" Bullet said.

"I know I got it. Charge this to da game" Lex huffed.

How sad, Bullet thought. Lex and his posse was going to their demise all over a pair of knockoffs you could buy at any local gas station or liquor store. When the bus arrived, Lex and his crew rushed to the back of the bus. Bullet took a seat in the front. Not because he was afraid, but because he didn't want Rosa Parks' boycott to go in vain. She didn't take being ridiculed and labeled enemy of the people' for nothing.

Lex rung the bell at his stop on 27th & Roosevelt Avenue. Bullet had long passed his stop. Most of Lex's crew had departed at their designated stops, except for one. He and Lex got off on the same stop. Bullet pulled the string for the next stop. Observing the area once off the bus, there wasn't many people around the apartment complexes. Only a father playing catch with his son that appeared to be no more the five or six years old.

Following Lex and his homies into the alley, Bullet drew his blue steal .38 snub nose, brandishing the weapon behind his right leg. Lex and his friends was caught up in a futile conversation. They din't see it coming. Bullet fired the shot and Lex felt the hollow point blasting half his face off. The glasses exploded in bits and shards, destroying the gaudy specs. Lex's body hit the ground like a sack of potatoes. Blood gushed all over the concrete.

"Don't shoot!" his buddy instantly pleaded, throwing his hands up.

"It's too late for dat. Tell God I said hello" Bullet replied. With no mercy, he squeezed the trigger three times. The bullets erupted blowing off the top of his skull. He emptied the remainder of the cylinder into Lex, then walked off leaving behind yet another unsolved homicide.

"On da gee, I'm on that with whoever want some. These bitch ass niggaz think it's sweet out here" Parlay ranted and raved. They'd been beefing with Dime Bag lately. Parlay could only assume they were responsible for Gunplay's murder.

"Revenge is a dish best served cold, and I'm servin' up cold cuts" he continued. "When I find who did this, Imma make his momma cry" he swore.

"What's understood needs not to be explained…" Bullet tried calming Parlay. There was too many ears around, and Bullet didn't want anyone getting wind of their plot. "I got a relatively good idea who did this" he said.

"Then let's ride with our Chinese friends' chopsticks" Parlay said.

"Let's take a ride and let me holla at cha" Bullet threw his arm over Parlay shoulder and they walked off with murder dwelling in their minds.

* * * * *

"Sis, it's time we switch da game up and elevate to a whole 'nother level" Cam'ron proposed. "You and I know da dope game gravy, but that dog food sauce" he said.

"I hear you bro, but I'm not sold a hundred percent. I'm not sure I wanna change da game..." Keys said reluctantly. "Yo know that heroin bring a whole lot of problems with it. Why you so adamant about makin' that transition?"

"Listen, sis" Cam'ron sat next to his sister. "We already got problems. That bitch ass pig Benson been breathin' down our neck from jump street. So, I figured... fuck it. Why half step? Let's go all in" he responded. Avarice was tantamount to pride. It was begotten a fall. Keys wanted to stay standing tall, and not come tumbling down like the Berlin Wall. So, she had to think before agreeing to it.

"I wanna be rich forever. What you think, Demon?"

"On some real shit, I don't give two fucks how we get da green" Demon informed looking up from his phone. "Like Baby Boy, guns and butta." The only thing Demon gave a fuck about was seeing the light drain from his victim's eyes.

"Money is money. How we get da money only relies on one's ambition" he said.

"I agree" Cam'ron seconded. "What 'cha say, Keys? Where do your ambition lie?"

Peer pressure is a bitch, Keys thought. It didn't influence her in the least. She was a boss, and she utilized the ability to orchestrate properly. Sudden moves were detrimental to their livelihood. To every action, there was a reaction. She played chess instead of checkers, making gambit moves in her decision making without being compelled to do the opposite.

"Bro, you know I'm all about a dolla-" she began but was interrupted by the chime of her cellphone. The display had an unknown caller. Normally, she wouldn't answer, but something edged her away from her better judgment. "Hello, who this?"

Demon's attention focused on Keys. In a matter of seconds, her pleasant expression turned to raging anger. "That bitch ass nigga dead!" Keys shouted, jumping from her seat and kicking over the glass coffee table. The glass shattered, and the appliances on it mingled in the fragments.

"Keys, what's up?" Cam'ron asked puzzled. Standing picking up the Remy bottle spilling over, soiling his plush carpet. Demon rushed over and wrapped Keys in his arms.

"They killed Candy..." she wept, wrapping her arms around Demon.

* * * * *

Ecstasy faded in and out of consciousness. Lights glared her vision, temporarily blinding her. People surrounded her on both sides in white coats. They wheeled her gurney down the hall.

"You're going to be alright..." was the last thing Ecstasy remembered hearing before drifting away.

Chapter Three

* * * * *

Black and gold oval Prada sunglasses concealed Keys' bloodshot eyes. She sat in the front row of Pastor James's church, Holy Redeemer. Sorrow and wailing could be heard throughout the church. Not a single tear had cascaded down Keys' face. It had been an entire week since her passing; and Keys cried herself out. All that was left was anger. To make matters worse, she was forced to listen to a sermon that had nothing to do with her daughter's life. Waves of fire surged through her veins like Dante's Inferno.

"Matthew 24:11." Pastor James gave scripture, serenading the masses. "Says many false prophets shall arise and shall deceive many" he preached. "Brothas and sistas, many of us right here in this sanctuary" he pointed out into the crowd from the podium, "have been led astray by the prince of darkness" he continued.

Keys was silent. It was obvious how the people provided the pastor with an opulent lifestyle. People were gullible and weak. They didn't realize God didn't need them. They needed him to make their simple lives have purpose. Keys didn't believe in God no more than she thought unicorns existed. She was a heathen. Pastor James didn't realize his meandering almost cost him a slug between them. Keys was tempted to pull her .40 Glock holstered to her thigh. She envisioned his lifeless body slumped over the podium. Blood cresting over the seeps spilling onto the maroon carpet. Rivers of blood pouring into the aisle like seas of holy water.

"We must not be led astray from da word of God..." Pastor James said. "John 3:16 says for he loved da word so much he gave his only begotten son for our sins. No matter what trials and tribulations we endure, it is only a test of our faith. Nothing leads us closer to God than atrocities."

At the conclusion of sermon, Keys sucked her teeth and squeezed her manicured hands. Her French tips dug into her palms, drawing blood. Keys rose to view Candy. She laid in her solid gold casket like a sleeping beauty. The mortician had done a good job making her appear life-like. Candy's make-up was on point, nails on fleek, and her Cassie hairstyle was swooped over perfectly. It appeared as if Candy was napping. Keys figured since Candy was top notch in life, she'd send her out in the same fashion in a chinchilla that fluffed out around her Christian Dior dress and matching red bottoms.

After the funeral, Cam'ron ushered Keys outside. They trailed in tow of the pallbearers carrying the coffin. Keys shuddered in the nippy whether. The day was morose, and the clouds were dark. Sort of how Keys' heart felt... like she was being blown in the wind.

"Did you make sure you put word out on da street I got a honeybun for anybody that know da whereabouts of Krazy and Bagz bitch asses?" Keys uttered to her brother as they walked down the stairs. Cam'ron gave Keys a knowing look.

"You know that" he answered. "Them bitch ass niggaz killed my niece, so them niggaz gotta go" he reassured her.

Cam'ron wasn't just talking either. In the last week, him, Hurk, and Demon had torn up the South side in search of Krazy and Bagz.

"I want to die in a grim fashion, even da devil a hide his" Keys' voice dripped with malice.

Demon and Big Hurk stood by the Benz limousine. Keys and Cam'ron stood on the steps watching Candy's coffin being loaded on the horse carriage. Keys went all out to give Candy an elaborate funeral.

"You look radiant in a dress and heels. You should dress like a lady more often" said Demon, eyeing Keys over. Keys smiled. She actually felt quite comfortable. Being her first in a dress and heels. It beat the hell out her normal tomboy look, jeans and Jays.

Tires squealed and came to a screeching halt. Keys looked up in the nick of time spotting a midnight blue Dodge caravan. The side door slid open, and two masked gunmen jumped out equipped with hundred round drums. Bullets dispersed and people begun to flee. Demon instantly pushed Keys down beside the limo to shield her. Demon released his twin .40 Glocks with drumsticks from beneath his Stacy Adams blazer, returning fire. Hollow tips rushed forward knocking chunks out the van. Hurk and Cam'ron took cover behind a

Porsche SUV. Keys removed her .40 from her thigh and fired over the hood. Bullets clanked against the fiber glass. During the pandemonium, the Persian horses startled and galloped away dropping the coffin off in the middle of the street. It hit the concrete with a heavy thump. Seeing this made something snap in Keys. She stood shooting wild. The mercenaries pushed toward her, at which time, Hurk inconspicuously crept around the van. Hurk placed the barrel of his 500 Magnum to the masked man's cerebellum and pulled the trigger. He blew his brains out through the front of his forehead. The other assailant took off and ran. Keys kicked off her heels and went after him. To no avail, he dove in the van and it sped away. "You dead!" Keys shouted after them.

Sirens wailed in the distance. Cam'ron snatched the limo driver's lifeless body out the front seat and took the wheel. The rest of the crew piled in and the bullet-riddled limo zoomed from the macabre scene.

* * * * *

"Faye, I don't understand what it is you want from me" Thug tried reasoning with her, pulling into the gas station on 35th & Garfield. "I can understand your concern. I should've called and let you know everything was everything. But understand, I'm a street nigga, and when da streets call, I gotta go" Thug tried his best to explain. Not that he owed her anything. Faye and him was only friends. She hadn't heard from him since she aided him. So, the least he could do was ease her mind.

"What I want for you to do is stop usin' me and show me da respect I deserve…" she replied.

"U-usin'!" Thug sputtered, biting his tongue to subdue his rage.

Faye was being mendacious. Thug had never used anyone. Since his grandmother's death, he'd took the harder way. "Look, I'll pull up on you later, that way we can discuss this face to face" he told her.

"Don't even bother" Faye hung up.

Thug sat in the car stunned for a moment. He was confused. They'd always been good friends. Now she switched roles and was acting like his lady. Shaking the flustering feeling off, he stepped out of the ride. Inside the station, he grabbed a bag of plain Lay's. Then headed to the cooler for a beverage. Thug collided with his cousin. He was in the aisle facing away from Thug. The cooler door was open with one hand, and he was lining his pocket with stolen merchandise with the other.

"What da fuck nigga, watch where da fuck you goin'!" Champ exploded, spinning around, he dropped and shattered a 40-ounce Ol' English.

"Or what?" Thug challenged.

"All my bad, cuz. What it do, family?" Champ's attitude changed looking up and noticing Thug.

"I should be askin' you da same thang…" Thug replied. "You up in this bitch like a kleptomaniac with your bum ass" he observed.

"Nigga fuck you." Champ replied. "I ain't stealin' shit. Who da fuck is you, Pink Panther? Move da fuck out my way" he charged by, bumping Thug's shoulder.

Thug paid him no mind. It was clear Champ was using false aggression to a boxing match. Champ had been that way ever since they were teenagers. Growing up Thug was a pauper, so weekends he spent with his auntie Shonda Williams because he was guaranteed a full course meal. When Champ had been caught in a lie, instead of taking responsibility, he wanted to initiate a fight. Thug shook his head. Thug chose a kiwi fruit Snapple and shook it up on his way to the checkout line.

"You have to pay fo yo drink!" the owner yelled in his strong accent.

"What drink, bitch?" Champ shouted back, in his mundane combative attitude.

"The one u spilled in the aisle" the owner said.

"Fuck you, I ain't payin' for shit. That shit was already there when I came in this low budget ass store" Champ stuck his middle finger up and stormed out the store.

Thug approached the counter and paid with a fifty-dollar bill.

"Keep da change. Take whatever buddy owe you out da extra" he said.

Outside, Champ leaned on Thug's hood, drinking a 40 ounce. It was clear his cousin was lost in the sauce. He was the only nigga alive that still drunk Ol', like it was still the 80s.

"Fam, yo ass need to grow da fuck up. Why da fuck you up in there stealin' 40 ounces like some old ass junkie?" Thug asked.

"Nigga, cause I can" Champ spat. "Why da fuck you all in my bizness? I do what da fuck I want" he ranted, pulling up his shirt to display his .9 Rugars on his waist. "You feel me, blood?"

"Chill, I ain't blood?" Thug asked.

"Alright loc…" Champ retorted.

"I ain't loc either" Thug replied.

"Well, it don't even matta. You heard what I said I am…" Champ prided, as if straddling the fence was valid. "Come on, let's burn rubber" he offered.

"Hell nah, I ain't goin' nowhere with your hot ass" he said.

"So, you dissin' me?" Champ fumed. "I should go in your pockets. If you wasn't family, I'd stretch your weak ass" he said.

Thug laughed and hopped in his ride. "I'll holla at' cha later" he chucked the deuces, smashing the gas. Thug couldn't take anything his cousin said seriously. He knew he was slow. Anyone with common sense could see Champ was a couple cylinders short of a ten speed.

* * * * *

Trouble, Roc'star, Gunna, and Wacko were all posted on the stop of the trap when Thug pulled up. He served a fiend six for the fifty that scampered up to him as he got out the car. He jammed the crumpled-up bill in his pocket as he approached his cronies.

"Sis, why you talkin' all this playa shit, how you be turnin' all this lil thoties out. You shouldn't have no problem lettin' me sample Cookie" Thug heard Roc'star tell Gunna as he walked up.

"Nigga, you must think cause you big bro, put yo ass down" Gunna demanded. "If any of you ever cross da line to deceive me, I'll put your ass out and drop you in da deepest part of da sea. Brotha or not."

Everyone laughed at Gunna's threat, though it wasn't to be taken lightly. Roc'star and Gunna were fraternal twins. Roc'star was 6'2" and 260 pounds with light skin, the tone he and Gunna had inherited from their father being black, and their mother being Puerto Rican. Anyone who wasn't in the circle would automatically be intimidated by his size alone. Roc'star was a killer, but not by instinct like Gunna. Gunna was a whole different entity standing 5'3" and weighing 140 pounds full of rage. If you even looked at her wrong, she'd shoot your eyes out. There was no doubt in their mind that she would put her on brother down when it came to her main dame. Gunna was over the hills in love with Cookie.

"Wuz da word, my boy?" Roc'star greeted Thug, ignoring his sister.

"Money, my nigga" he answered, showing everybody love. "Still out here chasin' a bag, and I ain't stoppin' until my figures countin' digits" he said.

"Amen to that" Trouble agreed.

"Where that nigga, Snake?" Thug enquired looking up the block. "I see his whip up da street" he said.

"He just got in with Toe Tag a couple minutes before you came up" Trouble said.

"So, I just missed him, huh?" Thug asked.

"Yeah, Tags said they had a money muv on deck. Knowin' Tags, you know what that mean" Trouble explained.

Thug nodded his head knowingly. Toe Tag was a gunner. The ultimate hood feral that got his kicks off body bagging oppositions. His characteristics were tantamount to Loc Dog of Menace II society.

"I hear you" Thug confirmed. "What up with 'cha, Wacko? You standin' over there all quiet. You makin' a nigga nervous" he said.

"You know me, fam. I ain't talkative" Wacko replied. Everyone present knew Wacko's silence spoke volumes.

"I do need to talk bizness with 'cha, though. A nigga runnin' low on da hard" Wacko told him.

"Speak, nigga. We all family here. Plus, numbers is my favorite topic" Thug responded.

"What 'cha got on you right now? I'm down to ball, no MJG" Wacko said.

"I gotta 63 soft in da whip. And it's that A1 butta wht 'cha need?" Thug asked.

"I got twenty-five on me, let me get that" Wacko pulled a go knot from his pocket.

"Come to my office" Thug said.

On the way to Thug's car, Diamond rolled up in her 2019 outrageous Range Rover. It flipped magenta and tomato red.

"Hey, daddy" Diamond said flunging her arms around Thug and passionately kissed him. "Where you been, beau? I haven't seen you in a while" she purred. Thug stood mesmerized by Diamond's unique beauty. She was a goddess. She was smelling food, like Tiffany & Co; and looking good dressed in a Louis Vuitton bird coat, and dress and matching heels that complemented her exotic feathers. She drove men crazy with her redbone skin tone, long mahogany ringlet hair, hazel eyes and Kim Kardashian's ass.

"You know how it is when da streets be callin' my name. Nothin' personal, I been busy" he told her.

"Too busy to come through and get busy..." Diamond sexually murmured in Thug's ear. "Come take a ride with me I got something to show you" she told him.

"Alright, let me handle this bizness. Go wait in da ride and when I'm done we can dip. Cool?"

"Always, baby." Diamond replied, kissing him on the cheek before strutting off.

"Damn!" Wacko exclaimed. "I wish that was in my DM..." he ogled her until she got into her car.

"For da right price, anything for sale" Thug offered.

Thug had no real attachment to Diamond. To him, thoties like Diamond came a dime a dozen. Her purpose for being around was to get green. So, if someone paid the right price, he would ask her to spread her thighs wide, for them to go deep sea diving.

Thug served Wacko, then hopped in shotgun with Diamond...

* * * * *

Toe Tag and Snake pulled into John Redhot's parking lot located on 27th & Center. Toe Tag quieted the high-power engine of his 2018 maroon and gold Charger that once sat on 26-inch gold and maroon Dalvins. He had took the rims off for the winter, and slapped the original factory back on.

"How you know buddy we here to meet?" Snake inquired, taking a pull from his Dagwood vape pin and inhaling the THC deep into his lungs.

"I don't." Toe Tag replied. "You know my brother, Vulture, and his main man's Rat, right?"

"I know your brotha Vulture, not that other cat" Snake replied.

Snake and Vulture had history. Way back before Toe Tag jumped off the porch and been baptized on the streets. He and Vulture was running around shaking the local dope boyz down. "Tell me, what your brotha and Cat's... Phats-"

"Rat" Toe Tag corrected.

"Yeah, Rat. Tell me wat he got to do with us meetin' with some nigga we don't even know?" Snake, rubbing his hand lightly over his waves.

"I overheard bro and em a few days ago rappin' bout some nigga they was plottin' on strippin'. I waited til bro was occupied and snuck ole boy number from his call log. Then hit em up and told him I need ten of them thangs" Toe Tag said.

"I hear you, but how you know that nigga ain't twelve? We can be walkin' right into a trap" Snake observed.

"Well if it is, we just gon shoot our way out like Queen Latifah on Set It Off" Toe Tag cocked his .9mm Biretta attached with monkey nuts. "We didn't come here to get acquainted with da nigga anyway. We came here to hit this sweet thang. And you know he sweet, how you gon do bizness with some niggaz u don't even know?"

Snake snickered at Toe Tag. It was true, but at the same time, they was doing the same thing. They didn't know. Still, Toe Tag humored him. He saw a bit of himself in Tags. Trained to go at any given moment. Now, he was grown and utilized his knowledge, wisdom, and understanding. Sort of how Niccola Machiavelli distinguished the act of a man and beast in the book The Prince.

Taking another pull from the Dagwood, Snake removed his .50 caliber Desert Eagle from his waist and placed it on his lap.

"My nigga, all I know is dead Presidents and body counts" Snake elaborated in the most eloquent way that he was all the way in. Ride or die.

Smuv pulled alongside of Toe Tag and Snake.

Toe Tag?" He asked rolling down his window. They'd had never met in person. Smuv had only heard of Tags through his brother.

"Yeah" Toe Tag confirmed. "Get in da back" he instructed.

Smuv grabbed his Prada bag off the backseat of his baby mother's 2019 Chevy Traverse and jumped in with Tags. "What's going on with 'cha?" Smuv made small talk climbing in the back seat. "Your bro has never sent anyone besides Rat. So, I'm a bit surprised he sent you on delivery. Your bro always preaching how he want to keep you out da game. What changed his mind?"

"Big bro and Rat's hands tied right now, so they sent me" Tags fibbed. "Let me see what 'cha working with" he said.

Smuv passed the bag over the front console. Toe Tags took a gander. When he opened the bag, the entire ride lit up and reeked of potent marijuana.

"That's wat'cha asked for, right? Ten pigs of Midwest's finest" Smuv asked leaning forward over the console between the seats.

"Yeah, that and them fly ass jewels you rockin'" Snake growled, smacking Smuv across the face with the heat. Smuv recoiled, clutching his bloody nose. The impact of the blow had broken it.

"Take this shit off!" Snake started removing Smuv's trinkets. He placed his knees on the front seat for good balance and kept his gun trained on him.

"Man, what da fuck?" Smuv asked in disbelief. He was astonished and mortified by what was taking place. Blood poured and seeped through the crevices of his fingertips.

Toe Tags opened the back door and dragged Smuv out by the collar of his Pelle coat. During the struggle Smuv produced a gun, and he and Tags went for it on the ground. When Snake came around the car, he slapped Smuv over the head with the butt of the gun. Smuv instantly balled up in a fetal position.

"Alright, man…" Smuv pleaded for mercy. "Take it… Take whatever you want, just don't kill me" he begged.

"Well today your lucky day cause we ain't gon kill your pussy ass" Snake assured, looming over him with his gun by his side. "But if I hear you out here on these streets like you on somethin, Imma put your ass down" he added striking Smuv over the head knocking him unconscious. They grabbed the merch and smashed Smuv, a bloody mess in the slushy snow.

* * * * *

"So, what 'cha gotta show me?" Thug asked.

Diamond parked in an empty garage behind an abandoned home on 36th & Galena.

"It's not so much what I want to show you, it's more what I want to do to you" Diamond seduced him, leaning over and licking his ear lightly, then biting his lobe. "I know da streets be callin' your name, so does this juice box" she coaxed.

Thug pulled Diamond close to him. They kissed and he pawed her ass. Diamond frantically unzipped Thug's jeans.

"I see you're excited to see me..." she breathed huskily, engulfing him in her mouth.

Thug rested his head on the headrest, as she took his ten inches down her throat. Letting his bulbous head rest beyond her uvula. She gagged adjusting her esophagus around his long meaty pipe. Then retracted and repeated the process.

"Eat da dick" Thug urged her, locking his hands in her hair as she bobbed up and down. "Yeah, like dat." He groaned. Her head pistoned up and down his pole, relishing his length.

"Mmmm, you taste so good…" she breathed, taking him in. She swirled her tongue around his balls, then trailed up the length and engulfed the tip. She worshipped his dick until he was forcing her to take him back in her mouth. She did so willingly, sucking vigorously. Thug watched her rapidly bop on his lap. She polished him regally. He began to fuck her face, pushing up into her succulent mouth with every licorice suck.

"That's enough" Thug said, pulling his dick from her mouth. It was mandatory he stopped her. The head was so good… if he didn't, he would cum in her mouth. "Let me see if you can ride this pickle betta than you eat" he told her. Diamond pulled up her dress and she didn't have any underwear on. She accommodated herself and descended on his stick.

"Mmmmmm…" she moaned heartily as he stretched her. "I been cravin' this all week" she said. When Thug was all the way inside her, she readjusted herself to fit him. Slowly she began gyrating her hips. Thug grabbed her waist and guided her to his liking. The windows started to fog up. Their fucking and kissing became feverish. She was bucking uncontrollably on his lap now. Thug matched her tempo pushing up into her as she rode him like a stallion. She wailed in ecstasy. Her body bucked and convulsed. Her copious juices coated his phallus, which triggered his own orgasm. As he splashed her insides, Diamond held him tightly as they came. She collapsed onto the seat, resting to catch her breath. Once she was composed, she started the car, and they headed to her home for round two.

* * * * * *

"Whoa…" Detective. Benson sighed in horror. Brown stared in dismay at the scene unfolding before his eyes. Benson parked their squad car at the edge of mayhem. They pushed their way through the bodies and crept under the yellow tape. Some were covered in white sheets, others in black body bags.

"If it ain't one thing, it's another" Benson said somberly. "Just when you thought you've seen it all, life has a way of showing you, you haven't seen the half of it" he said.

"Preach" Brown returned. "We barely got our nails dug into the last case. Now we have a mass killing on our hands. It's like the city never sleeps" he replied.

"Speaking of which, what's the analysis on the DNA samples we submitted?" Benson asked.

They'd been waiting for months to get results in the Jackson case. Benson had grown tired. Things must have been backed up in system. Normally, in a matter of weeks they would've had speedy results.

"The results came in this morning" Brown answered.

"And you didn't feel the need to tell me?" Benson said, seething.

"Hold up" Brown held up his hand. "Don't be so quick to jump to conclusions. You would've known sooner, but before I could update you, we got called here and it didn't cross my mind…"

Benson was satisfied with the explanation. It was logical, they'd been swamped with caseloads lately. Any man could've forgotten something so simple.

"Okay, any developments?" Benson further inquired.

"Yes and no" Brown answered

If Benson didn't know any better, he would've deemed his partner a moron, but Brown was just being himself, complicated as always. He always spoke in riddles or parables.

"The lab reports came back, but unfortunately there was no DNA match in our database. The only good news is the reports confirmed there are XY chromosomes in the blood sample. So, we know our suspect is male" he explained.

"So, in other words you're basically saying the perpetrator is a ghost?" Benson was irked. They still had no evidence leading them closer to solving the case. Surely it wasn't an elaborate crime. The assailant had been sloppy and careless by leaving shell casings and his blood on the scene. That was a rookie mistake. Technically, the case should've been solved within 48 hours. Unfortunately, the perp had managed to slip through the cracks.

"Well, yeah..." Brown confirmed. He wished he could provide more information, but the truth was in the pudding. The guy they was looking for was nonexistent. A figment of their imagination. "Unless you can produce evidence to prove otherwise. If not, this guy walks through walls" he concluded.

Benson starred lugubriously at a child's bloody shoe located inches from a body bag. Benson could only assume it was an unfortunate child at the wrong place at the wrong time.

"We'll touch base on that later. Right now, let's clean up this mess" Benson ordered. Brown nodded in agreement and headed in the opposite direction, leaving Benson alone to fight his own unwarranted guilt.

* * * * *

Ecstasy's ears perked up at the ABC news broadcaster. Turning her attention from the window, she wheeled around to face the screen wielded to the wall.

"We're outside the church of the Holy Redeemer..." the person announced.

Ecstasy grabbed the remote and turned up the volume.

"Where nineteen fatalities occurred, and eight others were injured after a shootout ensued. Witnesses say a blue Dodge caravan with the license plate number TMZ-666 pulled up after a funeral procession took place and two masked men opened fire. Witnesses say a third man was driving. If you have any information regarding the matter, please contact our local tip line. There is no report if any of the survivors are in critical or stable condition. We'll have more information at a later time. Thanks, you're reporting with—"

Ecstasy flicked off the television. A single teardrop fell down her face. She was incensed. Today she was scheduled to be released from the hospital. Her best friend lost her life right in front of her. But violence didn't cease there. Death lurked in the shadows. Candy couldn't even have peace in death. The only person Ecstasy wished more than anything to see dead, was Krazy. She vowed as long as she could breathe, that she would be the one to kill him.

Chapter Four

* * * * *

Tooley stepped into the bus terminal in downtown Milwaukee. A decade ago, he'd been convicted of a triple homicide back in 2009, and he'd done hard time until he found a loophole, an exploitation of a technicality that violated his Fourth Amendment. The U.S. Supreme Court had made a law-abiding ruling and vacated his conviction. Now he was back on the bricks like the red carpet had been rolled out. It was a new year and it was NBA- never broke again session. It was time to ball 2k19. Though it felt incredibly good to be free from the belly of the beast, he still couldn't shake the dreaded feeling he was leaving behind some real niggaz. Like Jambazi, World, Chaka, Diamond, and Ghana. He would look back and keep their canteen straight and get them an attorney to fight the powers that be. He still felt strange.

Tooley observed his surroundings. To be aware was to be alive. There wasn't many people occupying the bus station. It looked like Donald Trump's inauguration. Tooley locked eyes with a snow bunny that was gawking him from across the room. She wasn't bad looking with a slim waist and thick thighs. She was definitely a catch.

"I've seen flowers before, but I didn't think I'd see one here" Tooley spoke, his pull up game proper. "How you doin'? I'm Tooley, and you are?" he introduced himself, extending his hand for a handshake. She smiled warmly and took his hand.

"Hi, I'm Kelly" she answered, her cheeks blushing pomegranate. "Nice to meet you" Kelly said, checking out Tooley's immaculate attire.

A smirk creased the corner of Tooley lips. He noticed her observation. He was fresh, dressed down from head to toe in Mauri, but it wasn't the fashion statement that secretly made her panties cream. It was his alluring feathers. Tooley was handsome. Caramel skin tone, shoulder length dreads, and a manicured goatee. His six-foot frame was also well put together from long hours he spent in the gym up north. "No, nice to meet you" he beguiled, kissing her hand.

Kelly almost melted. Tooley's game was too strong to resist.

"Where are you from?" she asked, blushing and beaming with glee.

"From down under-" he began.

"You make it sound as if you're from hell" Kelly interrupted.

"Da right devil can turn hell into paradise" he cooed.

"Oh my, a bad boy at heart…" she smiled, fanning herself.

"In da flesh" he bragged, teasing her.

There was no doubt in Tooley's mind Kelly was experiencing hot flashes.

"Not to be a burden, but I'm new in town" Tooley lied, he was born and raised in Milwaukee. "May I use your phone?"

"Oh, that's no problem, here" she replied passing him her cellphone. "Take as long as you like" she offered.

Tooley smiled at how affable—and gullible—she was. In the hood, those actions were detrimental. Everyone had some hidden agenda.

""Wuz up?" Krazy answered on the second ring. "Who this?"

"This Tooley, wuz poppin'?"

"You know, same shit different toilet." Krazy huffed and cleared the phlegm from his throat. "Wuz up with 'cha? Why you callin' me from this unknown number? What ain't no money on the line, so you hit me three way?"

Tooley guffawed at his boy million and one questions. "Nah, ya boy out here on da bricks. I'm down here at da bus station. Come get me" he said.

"Nigga, you bullshitin'" Krazy replied astounded. He couldn't believe his ears. "Fam I ain't an Xbox, so why you tryna play with me?"

"Da only thang I play is this street. Tooley "Now come get me, I ain't got all day" he said exasperated.

Krazy detected the seriousness in Tooley's tone. Being in the cell with someone for years, you get to know them. That's how he knew Tooley was dead serious.

"Alright, I'll be there in twenty" he said, then hung up.

"Gratitude, I appreciate your kindness" Tooley graciously gave Kelly her phone back.

"Like I said, no problem" she repeated, sticking her phone in her coat pocket. "Why don't we head over to the food stand, so you can write my number down?"

"Nah" Tooley declined humbly. "I don't think my BM will be receptive to me politicin' with someone that's not her" Tooley turned on his heels and strolled away, leaving Kelly with her mouth hanging open...

* * * * *

"Fam, get in da backseat." Krazy demanded Bagz as they pulled in front of the bus station. "Let homie ride in da front" he said.

"Cool" Bagz didn't protest. He got out and climbed in the back. "But how you just gon pick buddy up in this hot ass whip, like that bitch Keys ain't got half of Milwaukee lookin' for us?" he asked concerned.

"Nigga, I wish you would shut da fuck up sometimes. Why you always thinkin' like a pessimist?" Krazy reproached, beating his fist on the steering wheel.

Krazy found it fishy Bagz was always speaking on Keys' name. He was starting to wonder why. "You think I really give a fuck about that bitch Keys and her weak ass henchmen? That bitch betta be easy give her a fourth hole right between da eyes" Krazy was a misogynist, and in Milwaukee, the city that never slept, hoes got it too.

Tooley tracked through the snow and got into Krazy's ride.

"Long time, no see" he greeted once seated. "Damn, it feel good to be back on da streets" he said.

"I know it do" Krazy agreed. "I was just rappin' with this scary ass nigga back there" Krazy pointed toward the backseat with his thumb, then pulled into traffic.

"Why don't you tell em what's really good?" Bagz insisted.

"Who is this anyway?" Tooley inquired. "And what is he talkin' about?"

"That's my boy, Bagz, my right-hand man I was tellin' you about" Krazy answered.

Tooley watched Bagz through the side view mirror. He had seen him in countless pictures Krazy had sent him over the years. Krazy kept it solid, unlike what Tooley could say about most. But then again, there was no comparison. Tooley knew that from the moment they were bunked up North. It wasn't much about Tooley taking a liking to someone, but Krazy was exceptional. He proved to be a hundred by staying true to his word, that he'd look back after his release. Every month, he filled his canteen, kept the phone juiced up, pictures, and laced him with new contacts of lady friends.

Whenever Tooley called, and needed something handled, it was done, no questions asked. All that made him too real to be cloned.

"What I'm talkin' about" Bagz angrily retorted. "Is that bitch Keys, and her boys lookin' for us, and we out here like we ain't got no worries. Ridin' in da same hot ass whip, like da streets don't have eyes and ears. Niggaz out here know who we are. How we know one of them niggaz or hoes tryna make a quick buck want rat us out? We need to be low-key" he ranted.

"Low-key?" Krazy mocked, offended by Bagz. "Nigga, I ain't got no worries, I'ma gee-"

"Hold up, be easy a minute" Tooley cut in. He was dismayed by the news he was hearing "You mean to tell me that bitch Keys ain't slumped?"

"Nah, family, I trumped that's bitch daughter first" Krazy explained. "Then I tried to double back and knock that bitch out at Candy's funeral service... But we missed. And I lost a good nigga in the process" Krazy stared off into the distance at the stop light. Chop had been his childhood homie, and he was missing him dearly. In silence he gave condolences, hoping Chop rested in peace.

Tooley closed his eyes and took a deep breath. The information stressed him out, so he leaned his head against the console to clear his mind. There was no need to verbally express his disappointment. This was a man's game. He knew if he wanted to claim his rightful place on the throne, he couldn't send a boy to handle a man's job. This was something he'll have to handle himself. "Y'all strapped?"

"Always" Krazy assured, removing his two Desert Eagles from his hip and placed them on his lap. "Why, wat up? I don't never go anywhere without my two friends, itchy and scratchy" he said.

"I need to make a quick detour before you drop me at baby momma's crib" Tooley informed. "I need to tie up some loose ends..."

* * * * *

Demon, Cam'ron and Hurk kicked in Chop mother's door and had everyone stretched out on the floor.

"Tell me where da fuck Krazy and Bagz is" Demon demanded, gripping Chop's mother by her weave. His P90 Rugur jammed down her throat. "Or I'll kill everyone in here" he threatened.

"Please..." Ms. Jones cried. Her sobs muffled by the cold steel. "I don't know what you're talkin' about…"

"Bitch!" Cam'ron snapped, slapping her across the face with His FN. "Don't play dumb. How da fuck your son end up tryna clap us at my niece's funeral and you don't know nothin'?"

Ms. Jones was on the floor groaning in agony. Demon pulled her from the floor and leaned her against the wall. Blood poured down her face, from a fresh gash over her left eyebrow.

"Now Imma ask you one last time, then pop goes da weasel" Demon threatened, cramming his gun back down her throat. "Startin' with ole grams" he retracted his gun and aimed it at Ms. Parker, who was hog tied and with fear in her eyes. She feared for herself, kids and her grandchildren who were all tied.

"P-Please d-don't!" Ms. Jones sputtered. "I told you I don't know who you're talkin' about. I didn't know anything about my son life or what he was into. Please, let me go. I just want to bury my son" she begged.

"There'll be no need to bury him, 'cause you'll meet him in hell" Cam'ron harshly said and pulled the trigger. Ms. Parker's head cracked open and blood splattered all over the shivering children.

"Ooooh, Goood, noooo!" Ms. Jones wailed. Streams of tears ran down her face.

"Shut up, bitch!" Cam'ron ordered.

Ms. Jones' body slumped over on the living room floor. Her blood soiling the oriental rug.

"What da fuck!" Hurk boisterously entered the living room, after conducting a thorough search of the home to see if any drugs, money, and if anyone else was hiding in the house. "Keys said no bloodshed" he said.

"Nigga, shut da fuck up" Cam'ron barked. "Keys ain't callin' da shots here, I am" he asserted. "I made da executive decision to make it a blood bath. Now do your due diligence and get rid of them brats" he ordered, then he and Demon left to wait in the car.

Hurk didn't argue. Deep down, he knew Cam'ron held some deep-seated resentment towards him. Hurk felt Cam'ron held him responsible for Candy's death. Hurk couldn't say for sure, but his gut told him Cam'ron felt he could have saved her. After all, that's what Hurk was there for, to watch over Candy to make sure the process went smoothly. Unfortunately, it didn't. Eer since that dreadful day, the vibe between him and Cam'ron had been off. Left with no choice, Hurk looked at the children and pulled the trigger twice.

* * * * *

"What makes you think buddy holdin' more than what you seein'?"

Trouble, Snake, and Toe Tag had been in the trap all day. Thug had dumped a four and a baby and was on his way to re-up. When Diamond showed up and proceeded to put them on a new sweet thang, she had them suckered in.

"Regardless, if its more or not. We goin' in to get that money" Diamond had informed them her stain had a quarter of a ticket in a book bag last time she was with him. That was too tempting to pass up. "I'm just tryna figure out what gave you da impression, dis nigga Yayo might have a half a ticket?" Snake asked.

"I understand your doubt." Diamond sympathized. You ever heard da analogy where there is a white spider, there is a hundred more? Not even that, da man got more jewels than Slick Rick. He pieced up like he some NBA player or rapper. I'm sure if he counted out two-hundred and fifty thousand, then he got a stash hid" she explained.

"That shit can be a fake like you" Trouble barbed. "How we know it ain't custom jewelry?"

"It could be. But one thang for sure he ain't got no baby dick" she shot back defensively, wagging her pinky finger.

Toe Tags and Snake erupted in laughter. Diamond and Trouble were like cats and dogs at times. Always toying and ridiculing one another. Under the surface, it was abundantly clear they had sexual tension between them, but their constant feuding prevented them from acting on it.

"Shut that shit up!" Trouble exploded. "It ain't even dat funny, and you niggaz over there cacklin' like a bunch of bitches" he snapped, disrespecting the homies. This was a major violation. You never called another man a bitch unless you were ready to fight.

Toe Tags and Snake cracked up. The laughter only added insult to injury, which bruised Trouble's ego.

" You must want me to put your ass down..." Trouble snapped at Toe Tag.

"Try it!" Toe Tag didn't back down, pushing off the wall with his foot, and came towards Trouble.

"Nah, it ain't finna go down like that!" Thug intervened, stepping in between them.

Thug felt he was the only levelheaded individual in the room. Everyone was always quick to act like savages instead of being logical. Knowing when to hold them, fold them, and when to run.

"Y'all niggaz geekin'. It's Pringle gang. United we stand divided we fall. We only rise against those who raise their sword" Thug said. "Now shake hands and make up. It's all luv in here" he requested.

The two respected Thug's wishes and shook hands.

"Snake, check your guy" Trouble added. By him being a shit starter, he couldn't pass the situation by not having the last word. Trouble didn't really consider Toe Tag as part of Pringle gang. Toe Tag was Snake's friend and it created animosity between them.

"And for da record, you lil yellow Marge Simpson lookin' bitch, I gotta enough meat down here" he pointed to his crotch. "To go in your rear and out your throat" he added in some effort to regain some dignity. Diamond had scorned his manhood.

"Never mind all that" Thug said, waving his hand in the air to signal damage control. "Diamond?"

"Yes, my king" she answered lovely as a servant ready to appease.

"I want you to get as close as you can and see what ole boy really holdin. If he ridin' around with a quarter ticket in a book bag, then there has to be more where that came from" Thug said. "Relay all da information to Trouble and he'll keep me posted. Since I see you two already have chemistry" he threw a devilish smile.

"Whatever, Thug..." she blew his last comment off. Sometimes she hated his wry sense of humor.. He was slick with his underlined sarcasm, which she didn't mind because she loved him and would travel to the end of earth for him. "Imma let dat one go. You think you so slick. Tryna fix me and Trouble up on da low. Imma get out of before you make me mad" she checked her pink diamond bezzled L.U. Chopard and grabbed her purse. "Bye, beau. I still love you even though you think you slick" she kissed him on the cheek.

"Imma bout to raise up too" Thug informed, showing love and followed Diamond.

Jeff surprised Thug opening the door. He stood on the other side with his hand up preparing to knock.

"Well if it ain't my favorite white boy." Thug enthused, embracing Jeff.

Diamond squeezed by and waved farewell over her shoulder.

"Come in" Thug stepped to the side, inviting Jeff inside. "What brings you around these ways?"

"What da fuck dude cracker ass want?" Trouble barbed nastily.

Thug glanced over his shoulder at Trouble with disappointment in his eyes. Trouble was heading into the kitchen, and Thug felt the urge to slap him on the back of the head for his stupidity. When Jeff came around, money was galore, cause he spent well. Trouble's behavior definitely had to be addressed. Not only was it starting to get old to Thug, but it was also starting to get in the way of their finances.

"Never mind him" Thug shut the door behind him. "What's good fly for a white guy?" he joked, starring at Jeff's immaculate attire. He was dressed in a Ralph Lauren shirt, Daks slacks, and Saint Laurent shoes.

"Nothin' much" Jeff conveyed. "Since I was in the neighborhood, I thought I'd make a designated stop" he added.

"Sound like some cop shit to me" Trouble continued to spew insults.

Trouble couldn't help projecting his flamboyant hatred for white people. It was hereditary. His father was a founding member of the Black Panthers. Throughout Trouble's life, instead of being taught how the Black Panthers was about growth and change, he learned from his father all about the nefarious deeds white America had inflected upon the black man. So, without considerable separation, Trouble placed all white people in one category.

"So, what do we owe to this surprise visit?" Thug awkwardly asked, trying to keep good vibes, and ignoring Trouble hurling accusations of Jeff being police. Money ruled everything around Thug. Any man with sense could see Jeff reeked of money. Jeff removed his men's Dior beaded saddle bag from his shoulder and dumped the content on the table.

"That is fifteen large. What will that get me?" he asked.

Thug looked over at Trouble, who glared at the money. Thug had to put his plans on hold. Jeff had earned rights.

"That a get you a half a slab" Trouble chimed in.

In the end, money was always the motive for understanding.

* * * * *

Tooley hopped out of the truck and holstered Krazy's .44 Desert Eagle in his pocket. Pulling his shirt down to conceal the weapons handle that protruded from his pocket.

At Tooley's request, Bagz stepped out and joined him. Tooley wanted reassurance for himself the Bagz was solid and could hold his own. Tooley looked up at the sky. His eyelids drooped softly at the beaming sun. There was hysteria within. That could only be met with the malice of murder. Tooley wondered if murder still felt the same. Like the thrill of animalistic fear mixed in with courage. That adrenalin rush that only a killer could feel. He didn't know, but he'd soon find out.

"Aye, me and buddy bout to go up in here" Tooley leaned into the whip. "We'll be back in about ten- or fifteen-minutes tops" he said.

"Do your thang. I'll be right here" Krazy said and leaned back to relax.

Bagz rapped on the front door. Tooley stood to the side out of sight. Tooley hoped old school Rico still resided there. After a decade, there was a high possibility Rico could've relocated. Rico opened the door, and Tooley stepped around the corner and stuck his pistol in his face.

"Surprised to see me?" Tooley asked, forcing him back into the foyer. "I can't believe you still live here" he said. *Damn idiot*, Tooley thought. "Didn't think you'd see me again, did you?"

"What's this about?" Rico played dumbfounded.

"What's this about?" Tooley mocked sarcastically.

In a swift motion, Tooley slapped Rico across the face with his pistol. Rico fell through the living room floor and hit the table. Glass shattered beneath his weight.

"Nigga, don't play stupid!" Tooley shouted. "You know damn well what this is about. Where my muthafuckin' money at?"

Tooley's blood was boiling. Before he had been apprehended, he'd left Rico with his stash. At the time, it seemed like the right thing to do. After ten long years without hearing a word from him, or not receiving one single zed, he had to reconsider.

"What's goin' on out here?" they overheard a young lady stepping out of the bedroom, cradling a baby. "What are you doin' to my dad?"

"It's okay Alisha." Rico answered, trying to remain courageous in the face of death. He sat up amongst the shards of glass and warned her off with his hand. "Go back in da room with my grandchild" he said to her.

"Nah, that won't be necessary" Tooley said. He had different plans. "Come take a seat on da couch instead, so we can catch up for old times' sake" he ordered.

She slowly walked across the room and kneeled by her father, watching how Tooley's gun followed her.

"I said on the couch!" Tooley barked, snatching Alisha up, and slinging her with her baby in arms, onto the sofa. "Bagz, search da rest of da house. I don't need any more surprises" he shouted.

Alisha sat silently, rocking her frazzled child on her knees. Tears streamed down her pretty little face. She couldn't believe they were being held at gunpoint.

"Long time, no see, Alisha" Tooley mused. Tooley had known Alisha since she was a little girl. They'd met when Rico had taken Tooley under his wing as an apprentice to show Tooley the ropes. It was the alternative to keeping him out of trouble. Back then, Tooley had been wild, committing unnecessary crimes like stealing cars and shooting at any moving target. He and Alisha became good friends. She had been his first love. She had grown far from the flat chested, flat assed little girl with the pretty face he once knew. She now had voluptuous breasts and a curvaceous ass. "My father didn't have anything to do with you goin' to jail Tooley..." she sobbed.

"I know that" Tooley retorted. "Your father knows exactly why I'm here. Why don't you tell her?"

Rico refused to speak. He sat on the floor looking helpless, no longer resembling the strong, relentless man Tooley once knew.

"That's okay. You ain't gotta speak, I'll tell her" Tooley insisted. "Your father stole a hundred thousand from me."

"A hundred grand!" Alisha gasped in shock. "Why didn't you tell me about this, dad?"

"I didn't want to involve you" Rico sobered up.

"Dad, I'm already involved. Da least you could've done was give me a heads-up, so I could've protected myself. Now look, me and your grandson involved" she screamed.

"I know, baby!" Rico sobbed. "I did it for you, though. How did you think I opened da specialty boutique? I did so out of those funds so I could set aside enough money to pay for your tuition just in case you decided to go to college after high school" he elaborated.

"Enough of da family history" Thug spoke up, grabbing Rico by the collar of his shirt and pulled him off the floor. "You can discuss family matters another time. Take me to my dough. And don't try nothin' stupid either, or I'll give you a part in your linin'" he threatened, shoving Rico forward.

Bagz returned and said the house was clear.

"Alright, grab mother of Jesus over there" Tooley ordered.

Rico's hands and arms were cut open pretty badly. Blood dripped onto the floor as he led the way. He led them into a dimly lit, damp basement. A space between the washer and dryer led to a room filled with boxes. Rico pulled a valise from behind a large pile.

"It's only forty-five thousand in here" Rico said, unzipping the suitcase. Bundles of money were revealed. A Tech 9 laid on top of the bills. "All I ask is you spare me and my family" he begged.

"That's like a slippery slope" Tooley confronted him. "If I let you get away with your treachery, everyone else will think they can get away with it too" he explained, aiming and pulling the trigger. The bullet hit Rico between the eyes. His body fell against the brick wall and slid to the cemented floor. Alisha and the child let out a screeching scream in sync. Bagz .took out his .40 Glock and Alisha was silenced by three to the chest. Tooley swooped up the hollering misfit and his suitcase. With them both in hand, he stepped over both heap of bodies and headed up stairs. Stopping at the stove, he turned the oven a full 500 degrees. He placed the child inside, shut the oven door, then headed out the front door with Bagz in tow. Tooley placed the money in the backseat, and more gunshots rang out. He took cover and grabbed his gun off his hip. He was about to fire, when he looked through the backseat and saw where the gunshots had come from. Krazy stood over Bagz.

"This is a man's world" Krazy said holding the smoking gun.

"What was that all about?" Tooley asked as they fishtailed from the scene. "Why you smoke ya boy? Fam was kinda alright?"

"Something told me if that bitch Keys got to him me, he would sell me out. So, I tied up da loose ends" he answered as they scrammed.

Chapter Five

* * * * *

"This boy always late..." Faye huffed in frustration. She glanced at the time on her iPhone for the umpteenth time. Thug had promised her he'd be at her home at one o'clock. It was twenty after one and he still hadn't showed. "I don't know why I waste my time with his ass..." she sighed, taking a sip of her Chardonnay she was nursing for the last half hour.

"I don't know either" Cookie replied. "You should let me luv you..."

"That'll never happen" Faye rebuffed.

"Don't you mean again?" Cookie coaxed her.

Faye and Cookie had been long term friends. Ever since sixth grade. They'd been thick as thieves. Back in high school, during their sexual experimentation, Faye allowed Cookie to convince her into going down on her. Faye wasn't gay, so she never returned the favor. Being a carpet muncher wasn't Faye's forte; so, after the second time, she never fucked around again.

"You used to let me taste you back in high school..." Cookie went on, sliding over next to Faye. Faye sat with her knees under her on the sofa.

"You can't tell me I didn't used to send you orbitin out of space them late nights in your bedroom. Tell me what man has ever made you feel as good as I did?" Cookie asked.

Faye felt found herself reminiscing about those nights while looking into Cookie's eyes. Cookie was an extremely attractive woman. Fine high cheek bones, full lips, and a scrumptious body. Her measurements 30-24-40.

"I used to make you call out. I had to cover your mouth with my had to muffle your pleasure, so your mother wouldn't hear us in da room next door. Remember that?" Cookie whispered, leaning in and kissing Faye on the lips. Faye reciprocated, their tongues dancing around, feverishly slithering in and out of one another's mouths.

"Stop!" Faye panted, returning to her senses. "Gunna will kill me if he knew I'd just let you kiss me."

"Gunna ain't gotta know. This between you and me" Cookie purred.

"But I'll know" Faye remained firm in her decision. "You gotta go, I can't cross that line with you again" she said as she pushed Cookie away and stood up.

Faye's doorbell rang. When she opened the door, Thug stood there with a bouquet of Cherokee roses, a card, and a teddy bear.

"I came baring gifts" he said as he extended them to her, smiling charmingly.

"Hmp." Faye huffed and flounced away. "Even the Wisemen showed up on time. And they didn't have a watch back then, they had to follow a north star..." she said sardonically.

"We alright, gurl?" Cookie asked for reassurance on her way to the door.

"Yeah, we good" Faye and Cookie hugged. "Call me later" she told her.

Alright, gurl. Bye, Thug" Cookie said closing the door behind her.

"So, you gon take your presents?" he asked.

"You might not be able to tell time, but at least you remembered my favorite flowers" she replied.

Faye grabbed the bouquet and gifts. She was shocked that Thug even remembered what flowers she liked. It had been a long time since she told him which ones. On her eighteenth birthday, they were on her back porch drinking and smoking, gazing at the stars. Thug had asked what kind of flowers she liked. She told him, giving a piece of history as to why. Being biracial, her father was black and her mother full-blooded Cherokee. It was a story her mother always told her growing up. One that never let her forget her heritage: The Europeans raided the Cherokee reservation heinously killing and savagely raping their women. The men fought back strong and hard but were short in manpower. So, the men forced the boys into battle, since they wouldn't allow the women to fight. Sadly, they lost, and the women shed many tears for their losses. The next day, the very spot where they had mourned their dead, a beautiful flower sprouted. It was called the Cherokee rose. Hence the story, is why Faye love the flower dearly.

"What up with all da sass?" Thug was perplexed. "You been talkin' out your neckline for a lot lately" Thug had mastered the ability to control his composure long ago. Which is why he'd never blown up. On the streets, that was a great quality to have. He ran into niggas false geeking all the time. He had to applauded himself occasionally for walking away from those types and not leaving a nigga stiff.

"You just gonna use me until I'm all used up?" she blamed. "When are you gonna see what is right in front of you is the real deal? And stop ignorin' what could be?" she said, facing Thug. Her eyes searching his, a technique many women did because the eyes were the window to the soul.

Thug's perspective of the situation changed. It had become clear as day to what Faye wanted and why she was acting out of character. Before his grandmother's passing, she had always told him to be aware was to be alive. Thug pulled Faye into his arms and kissed her. She didn't resist. Instead, she reciprocated passionately. Things got heated; clothes began to drop. Before long, she was divested on the kitchen counter.

"Oh, God, I love you Thug…" she breathed as Thug lightly kissed her shoulder blades. Making his way down, he paid a great deal to her erect nipples. She moaned and wretched in heat on the counter. Her pussy was sodden. Thug could smell the aroma of her arousals polluting the air. So captivating and ripe. Thug licked around her hillocks. She threw her hands above her head, bits of pleasure emitting from her mouth. When his tongue touched her clit, it was like a fire ignited in her. Her clitoris pulsated for release.

"Oh, God, eat me..." she chanted and begged. "Please, I need it..."

Thug took the encouragement. Her hips began to rock, and he grabbed her hips, to prevent her from doing more frantic humping, and attacked her clit. In moments she was cumming, soaking his face in her release. When her orgasm subdued, Faye slid to the floor and took Thug in the warmth of her mouth, relishing the bulbous head before taking him down to the base.

"Damn... you do that well..." he exclaimed, complimenting her techniques.

Faye had no gag reflex, she swallowed his ten and half inch missile down like a pro. Thug stood paralyzed, transfixed as she swallowed him whole.

"That's enough..." he said as he pulled his dick from her mouth and bent her over the counter. Her walls were slick as he pushed into her. Filling her to the halt with one thrust.

"Aaaaah, yeeessss! Ooohhh, fuck me!" she demanded in a sultry tone.

He filled her to the brim. She was a tight fit like OJ's glove. As he began to piston in her, her walls contracted around him.

"Damn, this shit good..." he groaned. "If I'd a knew this would be like heaven, I would've tried landin' here years ago..." They both laughed. Sounds of flesh colliding echoed throughout the kitchen. Thug was fucking her thoroughly. All Faye could do was hold on to the edge of the counter for dear life as he rammed into her full throttle.

"Yes, yes, yes, oh yes..." she repeated over and over.

Every time he ran up into her, he rocked her boat. The underside of his phallus hitting her G-spot. The pleasure became too great, and she came in a rush.

"Fuuuccck!" she wailed, overwhelmed as she came in rivers.

She coated his pole in her copious release. So much it ran down her thigh and his legs. He busted in her, filling her with globs of his semen. After he finished, Faye dropped to her knees and took him into her mouth and started the process all over again.

* * * * *

Benson and Brown arrived on 33rd & Cherry. Fleets of nosy neighbors crowded outside the yellow tape, all on top of cars, and porches. Benson observed around. There was no familiar faces and nothing seemed off kilter. Scrutinizing the scene was a routine every benevolent detective did. Sometimes the assailant adored returning to the crime scene to admire their work.

A white police sheet covered a victim on the sidewalk. His hand and foot stuck out from beneath the covering. The fire department had recently extinguished the fire. The home had been charred. Instinct told Benson he had a pyromaniac slash psychopath on his hands, but he wasn't sure. Hell, he could never be sure. Their entire occupation revolved off hunches.

"Can you tell me how the fire was started?" Benson approached Becker.

Kevin Becker was a fireman. Benson had known him for nearly a score. Twenty years was a long time to know a person. They'd been good friends since their college days, where they both dedicated their studies to law.

"In my opinion" Becker started sorrowfully. "The commencement of the fire has no germane. You should worry more about what you're up against here. Because there are many forces of evil dwelling" he continued.

"Alright, let me have it" Benson replied.

"There's two seared adult corpses in there, and the charred remains of an infant. The child's body was burned to a crisp. We had to pry its seared remains from the oven rack. We believe that's how the fire started" Becker explained.

"What?" Benson replied astounded. He was grimacing with peevish disappointment at the heartless, heinous act. "You mean to tell me some sick bastard stuck a child in the oven?"

""Yes..." Becker answered. "And turned the dial to the maximum. When we finally put out the flame, the damn child was damn near cremated. The child was burned so bad it looked like someone took a flamethrower to it. That's how badly this child was burned..." Becker's voice began to crack. He tried hard not to go into shock, but there was no use. He'd been in that line of work for fourteen years. Especially when confronted with the crimson, gruesome death he'd just witnessed. "I just can't fathom how someone could be so nefarious enough to cause a child such a horrible death..." he began to wonder if the infant had still been alive when placed into the inferno.

"Welcome to the party..." Benson said, more callously than he intended. "This is something you have to get used to..." he tried desperately to clean up his harshness. "There's been countless murders and deaths that make no fucking sense to me. Most of the time I end up with a bottle of Jack Daniels to whiteout the images and nightmares..." Most of the time, Benson tried to drink himself into oblivion. Doing so, his alcoholism had gotten far out of hand, putting a wedge between him and his family. Arguments became many. Until his wife packed up, took the children, and filed for divorce.

"Well, you're the homicide expert. So, I'll let you deal with the gruesome scene. Because I'm not going back in there" Becker said.

Benson's interest shifted. He focused his attention on the victim covered on the sidewalk. He wanted to know who it was, so he met back up with his partner.

"Any ID on the victim?" Benson asked, looking up at the sky. As if he expected an answer to descend.

"Yeah, I retrieved his ID from his pocket" Brown informed, passing the plastic credentials to Benson. A sense of hope washed over Benson. He gasped as he read the name card. It was Cashmere 'Bagz' Jackson. Bagz was one of the suspects wanted for questioning in the Candice 'Candy' Green murder.

"I think there is more than one assailant responsible here..." Benson alleged.

"What makes you so sure?" Brown asked.

"Well, for one, this guy here, along with his partner in crime, Krazy, was wanted for questioning. Which leads me to think this guy was hit to tie loose ends" he explained.

Word on the streets was Keys placed a bounty on Bagz and Krazy's heads. Benson aimed to get both of them off the streets before Keys could. Unfortunately, he was too late for one of them.

"Another thing is...." Benson continued. "Those two never got anywhere without the other. Which leads me to believe, whatever happened here, those two was involved. I just have to figure out how one of them ended up dead..." he said. "I want you to put an APB out on Kevin 'Krazy' Carter" he ordered.

"Okay, will do." Brown obeyed the directive and headed off toward their police cruiser.

* * * * *

"What up, who this?" Toe Tag answered his cellphone.

"This Smuv." the caller replied

"What 'cha want fuck boy?" Toe Tag hissed venomously. "Fuck you callin' my phone for?"

"Because I got a proposition. A solution to keep this beef to a minimum…" Smuv answered.

Toe Tag laughed. He found it ironic when he was the one holding all the cards

"Boy, yo ass funny. You can't come close to no giant. I'll hear your proposal, though" Toe Tag said.

"Bring me back my ice, and I'll call it truce" Smuv said.

"Nigga, go fuck yourself" Tags spat. "If you want them weak as jewels back, bring me sixty grand. Otherwise, don't call my line no mo" he snapped.

"This your final chance to come correct, or else it's war…" Smuv threatened.

"Well, then it's war" Tags accepted the challenge. "When you see me, let them thangs talk. You betta hope I don't see you first" he warned, hanging up.

Chapter Six

* * * * *

Yayo's 2019 Gensis G70 was parked in front of Diamond's residence. Diamond's head bobbed on his lap, engulfing his dick.

"Damn, girl, you tryna suck a nigga soul" he grumbled. His head rested on the window glass, and his lips parted slightly.

"I seen a dress to match them heels I told cha about" Diamond spoke briefly, removing his piece from her mouth.

Diamond knew the best way to trick a man into something was to pray on his vulnerability. Men were weak in the heat of the moment. When it came to sex, men were hard when they were soft, and soft when they were hard. By her being a vulpine, she knew this. "I think I'll look good in them tonight. Can I get them?" she coaxed.

"Yeah, yeah, yeah…" Yayo panted. "If you suck me right, you can have da world" he promised, shoving the back of her head downward. She took him back into her succulent mouth. Her lascivious tongue cradling the underside as she sucked him. She sucked with presto until Yayo disgorged in her mouth.

Rivets coated her tongue. As she sat up to reapply her make-up, she swallowed and licked her lips seductively.

"You da best" he appraised, zipping up his Balmain jeans.

"One good favor deserves another" she replied, holding out her hand. "Them heels cost fifty-two hundred" she told him.

"Damn, chameleon..." he huffed. Because her beauty wasn't settled, she could look different every day. "You didn't even give a nigga chance to recoup. Show a nigga some luv" he said. Diamond leaned over and whispered in his ear. "I just showed you some love. Now it's your turn to return da favor" she responded.

Yayo didn't argue. He dug in his pocket, fished out his cash, and counted seventy-five hundred.

"I also seen a purse..." Diamond added.

Yayo counted another three grand.

"Look, I gotta go" he said. He knew if he didn't get rid of her soon, she would talk her way deeper into his pockets. "I'll see you later on tonight. Be ready at seven" he ordered.

"Okay" she complied, sticking the dough in her Chanel purse. "I'll be ready" she replied, then kissed him on the cheek before getting out the car.

Diamond stood on her porch and watched as Yayo's taillights turned the corner. Then she called Thug. "It's on tonight." She spoke into the phone, then hung up.

* * * * *

Keys' yellow and black Bumblebee 2019 AMG pulled to the curb in front of Ecstasy's home. It was May 12th, Mother's Day. Crowds of hustlers were on the porch next door. One of them stopped Keys as she exited her luxury vehicle.

"Wuz up, sweet lady?" he said leaning over the fence that separated the two homes. "I'd choke a brick and kill a stick for a chance to get to know you" his words flowed smoothly off his tongue.

Keys gave him a once over. The local neighborhood hustler wasn't bad on the eyes. He was well groomed, had a rich chocolate skin tone, and he wore updated fashion.

"Maybe in another lifetime" Keys replied. She let him down easy, without any insolent words that would bruise his ego. She knew that didn't make a difference when she heard his guys laugh, and clown him for being dissed.

"Fuck you too then, bitch…" he retaliated. Keys paid him no mind. She was a boss, and everything the light touched was hers. She was a queen, and those under her reign kissed the ring. Her Monolos clicked on the pavement as she switched by the degenerate. Her Givenchy jeans fit her derriere, and her matching blouse contoured her figure. A woman of class never stooped down to the level of those beneath her.

"What up, stranger?" Ecstasy greeted, perched in her wheelchair.

Keys placed her multicolored Prada Saffiano Bandolier on the railing and hugged Ecstasy.

"Sorry I haven't seen you in a minute" Keys apologized. "Things have been so stressful. If you know wat I mean?"

"Yea, I know what you mean" Ecstasy related. It was clear Keys was referring to Candy's death. It hadn't been a walk in the park for Ecstasy to rid herself of the tragic day either. "Nevertheless, I need to teach myself how to walk again, so I can stretch my limbs" she continued.

Keys looked over her shoulder before taking a seat. She wanted to make sure it was safe to do so. You could never be too at ease when a man's pride was on the line. The degenerate was too busy with a customer to be worried about anything else.

"Yeah, them thangs is gettin' scrunny" Keys said and they laughed. "You want me to tie a string around dem noodles so I can manually walk you around?" Keys playfully smacked Ecstasy's leg. "Tell me how you been? How's your mom?"

"Everything, everything" she answered mildly. "Mom is an angel. A true blessing" Ecstasy enthused. "She been waitin' on me hand and foot. Makin' sure my cripple ass receive da proper treatment" she said.

"A mother's nature." Keys said, remembering her own.

She thought back on how Candy had been a child. Candy was a precocious little girl. She never gave any problems. Candy was heartfelt, caring, and smart. Keys found solace in the warm fuzzy remembrance. "Speakin' of mothers, I'm throwin' a bash next month on Candy's birthday in her honor" she told Ecstasy.

"What's that, June 16th?" she asked.

"Yeah" she responded.

"I still may not be able to walk by then. What you want me to do, roll up in there like Legs off Don't Be A Menace? On my gurl's birthday..." Ecstasy joked, pointing at her wheelchair.

Ecstasy was currently going through physical therapy too overcome her temporary paraplegic state. Monday through Friday, and she had made little progress.

Keys giggled at Ecstasy's silliness. Keys was glad in her condition she could smile, and still had a sense of humor.

"You can do whatever you want, Wheels" Keys teased.

More laughter erupted from the two. They cackled and went down memory lane for old times' sake. Suddenly, Ecstasy went quiet, and her face went stale. She stared out into space.

"What's up?" Keys asked with concern.

"Gurl, this situation really irks me. I can't forget what that bitch ass coward Krazy did. I want that bitch ass nigga's head so bad it makes my pussy itch, Keys..." Ecstasy's face was contorted with rage. "Tell me you got da drop on that pussy?"

"Calm down, gurl..." Keys rubbed Ecstasy shoulders. "Me and da team on da job. You ain't got to worry about shit but stayin' calm and focus on recovery..." Keys decided to keep under her hat that Bagz had already been whacked.

"Keys, I hear you. But I can't stay calm. I've been so mad, that I can't even focus on my college exams online. I don't even think I'm returnin' back to school. All I fantasize about is singin' that nigga da lullaby."

"I know you mad, Ex, but don't allow your anger compel you to make a mistake by droppin' out of school..." Keys advised. "Trust me, we got dis. We gon make sure dat muthafucka pay in blood" she avowed.

"Okay..." Ecstasy agreed. "I'll stay in school under on condition" she said.

"Tell me" Keys replied.

"When you get da drop on that bitch, I want to be da one to put him out his misery."

* * * * *

Thug's new Ducati 1260 motorcycle halted at Lincoln Park. He leaned the bike on its kickstand and helped Faye off the back.

"I appreciate our wonderful day" Faye expressed her gratitude in glee as they strolled through the park hand and hand. They stopped to enjoy the floral display inside the domes.

"It was time well spent" he replied. "You don't have to thank me. It was da least I could do. I'll do whatever for my queen. I'll give you da heavens, moon, earth and everythang in it" he said.

Faye smiled. They'd just finished enjoying a delectable gourmet brunch at Olive Garden and a matinée.

"I know, baby" Faye turned to face him. "But I still want you to know I'm appreciative for all the little things you do for me. Da last five months have been a good odyssey for me. And I just want you to know how much I care" she responded, standing on her tippy toes and planting a kiss on his lips.

"Lil sexy, it's your actions that show what you tell. I already knew that without you tellin' me" Thug assured. "I got an idea though" he said.

"What's that?" she asked.

"Let me romance them guts right here on da dome and make a sex tape" he suggested.

"Ugh, boy, nah" she swatted his arm. "Come on, and let's enjoy our walk, and quit thinkin' nasty" she responded.

"That's hard to do when I'm with you…" he teased her.

Faye swatted him again and they both laughed.

"Alright, alright…" Thug threw his hands up. "No more violence. Come on, let's walk" he slapped her ass. she jumped and swatted his hand. "Boy, you manège…" she laughed.

They were enjoying each other's company when Champ materialized. "Wuz up, cuz..." Champ slurred. It was clear he was inebriated. A liter of V.O.S.P. Remy dangled in his right hand and a lit blunt of Kush in the other. "What 'cha doin' ova er?"

"Shit, I was just about to ask you da same" Thug replied.

" Ya know me, cuz, I'm ubiquitous..." Champ said, not knowing his choice of words had nothing to do with the subject whatsoever.

"Did you just learn that word?" Thug ridiculed his cousin. Thug knew he was slow. Champ's IQ was lower than a sixty, which made him legally retarded. "Yay for da retarded kids..." he said.

If looks could kill, Thug would have dropped dead on the spot. Champ mugged grimly.

"Whatever fuck nigga." Champ replied. "I see you got some new eye candy on your arm. She not finer than that damsel Diamond, but that ass is fat on this hag."

"Watch out lil cuz. Guidelines, you ova steppin' boundaries. This wifey." Thug warned.

"Fuck that!" Champ grimaced. "You should've thought of guidelines b'fo you said that slick shit out 'cha mouth. What's up, lil ma? Why don't you dump this loser and run off with a winner? I got drink, I got weed, what up?" He went towards Faye and grabbed her ass.

Champ's actions set Thug off, hitting Champ with a mighty blow to the jaw. Champ went down like an anvil, fast and hard. Faye grabbed Thug. He could hear her yammering.

"Stop, stop, stop—!" she shouted repeatedly.

But Thug tuned her out. Thug straddled Champ, who was balled up on the ground, and began to punch him out.

"Babe, that's enough!" she begged, grabbing his arm, nearly dragging him.

Faye's voice resonated with Thug, drawing him from his zone, back into reality.

"It's alright, babe..." Faye soothed, holding Thug in her arms. "It's alright" she said.

Thug looked over and realized Champ was unconscious, his face was a bloody pulp. People begun to gather around with their cellphones filming it all. Thug took Faye by her hand and they rushed away.

Chapter Seven

* * * * *

Benson was sitting at his desk swiping through his tablet, viewing the gory murder scene. That one left more casualties than the Saint Valentine's Day massacre. He was trying to wrap his head around one single question: *why?* His partner strolled in the office. "There's a gift waiting for you in the interrogation room" Brown informed, standing in the doorway carrying a load of case files.

"Okay…" Benson acknowledged him. "I'll be there in a minute" he informed. Without uttering a single word, Brown nodded his head and dismissed himself. There was one casualty that haunted Benson. It was that of a ten-year-old child gunned down next to her mother. He could still see her bloody Nike shoes. It bothered him to the point of cold sweats. The child and the mother didn't deserve to be killed. The mother was walking her child to the corner store in 35th & Villard when the madmen pulled up at the funeral like it was a shooting range. Benson placed his tablet under his arm, took a deep breath to clear his head, then headed down the hall and the interrogation room.

"So, who's the famous speaker today?" Benson approached his partner and asked. There was always someone coming down to the station to volunteer information. With the tips, it really took the edge off his days, and made it easier to solve cases.

"Remember that case we were dispatched to about six months ago?" Brown asked. "You had a hunch Keys was connected to the homicides?"

Benson groaned at the thought and scratched his neck. "Yeah, because her son was one of the assailants that massacred all those people at Keys' daughter's funeral" Benson confirmed. The unsolved mystery had left Benson in many sleepless nights. First, the son dies at the scene. Then less than a week later, the family ends up slaughtered. If you put two and two together it equaled four. The only thing was Benson couldn't figure out was how Keys and her goons had gotten the family's address. "But what does that have to do with that matter? What, is Keys in there willing to talk?" he joked hopelessly.

"Not even close..." Brown chuckled. "On the contrary, the candidate inside can provide the information we've been looking for..." he said.

"Let's see" Benson replied, opening the door and stepped inside. "Hi, I'm-"

"I know who you are" Anthony Parker cut him off.

The man before Benson sat with his hands flat on the zinc table, nursing a Dunkin' Donuts coffee. His beard was grizzled and unkempt like he hadn't shaved in quite a while, and his shirt was wrinkled.

"You're the detect that's been investigating my wife and daughter' murder…" he said.

"Yeah, and you are Mr. Parker, right?" Benson asked.

"Yes" he answered.

"What brings you here today?" Benson asked, placing the tablet upside down flat on the table. He sat on a stool next to Brown. Anthony took a minute to gather his thoughts before answering while taking a sip from his lukewarm coffee.

"I'm here to finally talk and shed light on my family's killer, so they can finally get justice" he began.

Benson and Brown couldn't believe their ears. Back when the case was fresh, they couldn't pry information from him. Benson knew he was hiding something and used every tactic in the book to get him to fess up to help solve the case, but it was futile.

"What prompts you to do so?" Benson asked.

"I've had a lot of time to dwell on the matter, and I owe this to my late wife and child" Anthony's voice was strained and began to crack. Tears streamed down his face, and Benson offered him Kleenex, which he took, dampening the tears away. "If I didn't, God wouldn't have sent that angel to spare me and my grandchildren" he continued.

"How do you mean?" Brown asked.

"I mean one of the men that invaded my home that dreadful night, saved my life..." he sobbed.

Benson and Brown didn't say a word. They let him compose himself and continue to carry on.

"I believe da fellow name was Hurk. I believe that's what they called him" Anthony paused briefly to take a sip of his coffee. "I'd been upstairs asleep in me and my wife shared bedroom, when they forced their way into our home. When I heard this, I hid in da closet. I could hear them crying and yelling downstairs. Then suddenly it stopped, and I could hear them tell this fellow Hurk to check da house..." Anthony broke down and sobbed into his hands.

"It's okay" Benson consoled, rubbing the big man's back. "You'll be alright" he soothed.

When Anthony composed himself, he resumed. "Hurk found me. He told me to stay quiet and remain where I was. Then he left. A couple minutes later, I heard gunshots and then they were gone. I stayed in da closet cowering. When I finally worked up da nerve, I went downstairs, and found my niece and nephew alive and my wife and daughter dead" he sobbed profusely.

"We're going to show you an array of photographs, if that's okay with you?" Benson proposed. "See if you can pick out the photo of this man that you say saved you and your grandchildren's lives. Can we do so?"

"Yeah" Anthony nodded. "Like I said, I owe this to my wife and daughter" he said.

During the photo lineup, Anthony gave Benson and Brown both what they wanted. That left them with only one thing to do, which was obtain a search warrant.

* * * * *

"Hey, gurl!" Diamond shrilled answering her iPhone., looking out the corner of her eye at Yayo who was driving. "We on our way to my man's house. You know where he live…" she said.

"Ay!" Yayo shouted, his antennas going up like a deer in headlights. "Don't be tellin' people where da fuck you goin'. Who that on da phone anyways?" he questioned. Diamond rolled her eyes and hung up.

"Baby, don't be so uptight" Diamond leaned over and murmured in his ear and stroked his thigh. "That was my gurl on da phone, okay?"

Diamond knew Yayo was a sucker, so she used her feminine wiles to sate him. She knew how to coax a sucker well. Yayo smiled and put the peddle metal as her head descend into his lap. At home, Diamond savagely ripped his shirt off as soon as they entered his home.

"Damn, you feisty…" he breathed huskily.

"Only when I'm turned on. You look and smell so good. And I need you so bad." she vamped, unbuckling his Salvatore Ferragmo belt and pants.

Yayo picked her up and pushed her against the wall.

"This what 'cha want..." he said.

"Yes, daddy" Diamond cooed, pawing at his back as they kissed. Yayo pulled her panties to the side and slid into her. They both moaned in enjoyment. He roughly pushed inside of her. Her back scratched against the wall. "Yes, yes, that's it..." she moaned repeatedly.

Yayo was so caught up in the moment, he hadn't even noticed the masked men that crept into his home until one of them spoke.

"Look at those two pumping chump..." Thug barbed.

Yayo jumped, dropping Diamond from his grip as he scrambled to pull up his pants. He'd literally been caught with them down.

"Who-how—" Yayo stuttered. "How in da fuck did you get in here?" he asked. He'd been so caught up in the heat of the moment, that he'd forgot to close and lock the front door behind him.

"Why don't you ask your girl over there?" Thug waved his gun in Diamond's direction. She had her dress back into place and was standing quietly. "I'm da girl on da other end of da telephone" Thug said.

Yayo looked at Diamond and charged at her.

"You punk ass bitch!" he heaved.

Thug clobbered Yayo. He went down in a heap, grabbing his wounded head. Thug stood over him and pointed at his head.

"You know why we are here, so ain't no need to go through da motions" Thug said. "Fam, go with Diamond and get da cream" he told Snake.

He and Diamond went off and returned moments later with a book bag stuffed with cash.

"Fuck you, nigga, when I catch you I'm killin' you and this wretched ass chick..." Yayo threatened.

"Is that your word?" Thug struck Yayo over the head a second time, knocking him out cold. Fleeing, they all piled into the Expedition with Trouble behind the wheel, and they burned rubber, four hundred and twenty grand richer.

Chapter Eight

* * * * *

"Be careful tonight, babe" Jackie pleaded, hugging Trouble. They stood out front of their home in front of her marked police cruiser. "I don't want you gettin' in no mess tonight. I know you, and I don't want you gettin' hurt" she told him.

"Chill, baby" Trouble soothed. He was on his way to Keys' birthday bash. "Who would want to hurt a face like this?" he joked, turning showing his profile.

"You so conceited..." she laughed. "But I'm serious. You puttin' yourself in a lion's den. And I really don't want you to go. Why don't you stay home, and I'll call in sick. We can just lay back and watch a movie" she offered.

Jackie was a police officer. Over the years, she had seen the most heinous of crimes take place at clubs and bars. When liquor took effect, people's judgment became impaired and led people to commit stupid acts.

"If something cracks off tonight, don't be afraid to call. You know da police da biggest gang in America, and I'll have my boys on da scene pronto" she told him.

"Bring your ass on, lover boy!" Thug honked his horn and yelled.

Trouble waved Thug off over his shoulder and kept his attention on Jackie. Jackie loved Trouble for the way he treated her. He never was afraid to show his love and affection in front of company. He never faltered or changed up.

"Baby, I'm good" Trouble reassured her, pulling her close. "Plus, I'm a street nigga, what I look like lettin' my lady fight my battles? That a make me look weak as fuck, baby. You just stay pretty and being careful yourself tonight" he soothed.

"Okay, beau" she agreed. "I'll see you in da mornin' when I get off" she said, kissing him on the lips.

"Can't wait..." he replied and seen her off.

"What 'cha tryna rewrite William Shakespeare's with all your romance?" Thug teased as soon as he got into the car. "Damn, nigga, we gon be late because of you" he said.

"We supposed to be late, we da life of da party" Trouble said.

Thug put the car in gear and headed to the club. They rolled three cars deep. Snake and Toe Tag right behind, and Roc'star and Gunna in tow in their big boy Excursion.

* * * * *

It was a quarter to midnight, and club International was already packed with people from all walks of life. Keys and

Demon went through the masses, heading for the back room where Qubo Rodriguez waited. Keys stepped into the office and let the sound-proof door close behind her.

"Greetings, mi friend." Qubo greeted in his strong Colombian accent, standing to shake Keys and Demon's hands. "How's it ben? Long time no si…" he said.

Qubo had been supplying them for a decade now. He did good business, and he always had A1 product. Keys glanced around the room before answering. It was a force of habit, she always needed to know the exact count of people in her vicinity.

"There's no neet ta count." Qubo said. "I know wat ur up ta" he told her.

Keys stood quiet. She let out a nervous laugh before replying.

"I have no clue to whatever you mean" she said.

"Keys, I know you betta den you know yourself. You were counting da men in da room" he pointed out.

"You know me so well…" Keys guffawed.

She didn't mind Qubo had read her like an open book. He had always been a benevolent judge of character. Not to mention he had people in high and low places he could get information from whenever he needed. As a child, she had been diagnosed with OCD. That was information he had probably kept under his hat.

"How have you been, Qubo?" she asked.

"Livin' da high life, I can't complain" he responded.

"Believe me, I can relate…" she empathized. "But my brother here…" she walked over to the corner where Cam'ron stood quietly and tugged his arm. "Believes we need to elevate our game" she added as she led him towards the desk.

"How so?" Qubo asked, raising an eyebrow. "I thought you were already doin' quite good myself. So, tell me what troubles you with how your livin' ta'day" he offered.

"I'm not troubled by how I'm livin' today, but after good consideration. I want to expand" she said.

"An how do you propose we do so?" he asked, leaning forward in his seat.

"Heroin" she answered. "Before you reply, let me say our bizness has been very lucrative. We bring you a mil in a half, close to two mil a year. With what we propose, I can double that, possibly triple it" she continued.

Qubo pondered her words for a moment, then relaxed sitting back in his chair.

"Then let's talk bizness" he concluded.

* * * * *

Music blasted from the trunk of Diamond's Range Rover. Her two best friends Keisha and Tina cruised the boulevard looking for a place to park. People where everywhere, and it was hard to find parking space. All the ballers, pimps, and playaz had come out tonight. There was so many people waiting to get inside Keys' big Black Panther theme bash, those that weren't VIP had to wait in a line backed up all the way around the corner. That didn't bother the gold diggers that were out. Their hopes ran high, hoping they'd be spotted by a baller, so they could rile them in and hooked them on their line of bait.

"Gurl, it's lit out here tonight." Tina enthused from the backseat. "Look at all these walkin' banks out here. I'm finna be deep in some nigga pocket tonight" she said.

Diamond found a parking space in the parking lot and fit her Range between a Porsche Panorama and a candy painted 747 BMW sitting on 26-inch Dalvin's.

"Or some nigga gonna be deep in you" Keisha shot shade, as she stepped from the ride.

"You jealous?" Tina shot back.

"Jealous of what?" Keisha asked offended by the question. "Of you bein' a slut. Gurl, please. I don't need to fuck every nigga with a deep pocket. I'm self-made" Tina laughed at Keisha.

"You think that hurts my feelings?" Tina asked.

Tina and Keisha was always bickering at one another. They were always trying to downgrade one another to make themselves feel better. As if they were better by default. Keisha was no better than Tina. She had once been a stripper until she suckered her a baller, and he pulled her out of the life.

"That's probably your problem, you need somebody to tune this up" Tina said, slapping Keisha on the ass.

"Ouch!" she howled. "Damn, chill." she slapped Tina back on her backside.

"Y'all both need to chill" Diamond spoke up, hitting the alarm chirp to lock her car doors. "Can't we just have fun tonight?"

Her girls couldn't argue with the request. They all hugged and headed toward the club.

"Damn..." Diamond spat, stopping suddenly. "I left my purse in da car. Imma go back and get it" she said, walking back.

"That's okay, we'll wait for you" Keisha insisted.

"Nah, y'all go on ahead. I'll be fine catch u in a minute" she reassured them.

"You sure?" Keisha and Tina asked.

"Yeah" Diamond replied. "I'll see y'all in a minute. Just let me grab my purse" she said and kept walking.

Keisha and Tina went ahead, and Diamond went towards her ride. Her heels echoed off the pavement in the night. She was near her car when a blue Chevy sedan rolled up and a masked man jumped out the passenger side and stuck his gun in Diamond's rib cage.

"Get in da back" the man ordered. "And you better not scream or run, or you'll find out a bullet travels four times faster than da speed of light" he threatened, shoving Diamond in the car and climbing in behind her. The driver hit the gas, and the car vanished inconspicuously into the night.

* * * * *

Thug and his entourage stepped into the club a little after twelve o'clock. They were all fresh to death, and their pockets chunky. Thug rocked blue and purple True Religion and matching Louis Vuitton's sneakers with a Sandi Miller belt with an 18-carat white-gold monogram BG buckle flooded with six carat diamonds topped his outfit off.

They all went their separate ways in the club. Thug looked around before heading to the bar. There were black and purple ribbons all around the ceiling, stage, and doors. Black Panther balloons were in every corner, and naked painted bottle models danced in cages, carried trays and took orders. To top it off, all the screens had Black Panther playing on them. Keys had gone all out. Everyone looked to be having a ball, enjoying the party.

"Let me get a bottle of Jim Beveridge" Thug ordered at the bar. The waitress was a dime piece. She was chocolate, with full lips and a fat ass.

"It seems someone enjoys da finer tastes in life" Keys said, turning to face Thug.

"To whom do I owe da pleasure?" Thug asked.

"Well, that depends on whom wants to know" Keys answered.

"Your excellence" Thug said.

"Funny" Keys chuckled elegantly. "I could have sworn this party was thrown in da likeness of my late daughter, and she is my excellence" she said.

"I guess that answers my question" Thug acknowledged. "I'm speakin' with da infamous Keys" Thug looked her over. She was nothing like he had heard her to be. The streets described her as a tomboyish maniac. But she stood before him like nothing of the sort. She was dressed in a black Adam Lippes cocktail dress, matching Tabitha Simmons heels, Jacob & Co earrings and a David Yurman bracelet. Keys was beautiful.

"You're nothin' like they say, you flawless" he complimented, captivated by her beauty. "I've been dyin' to get acquainted with you. In fact, that was my mission tonight" he confessed.

"Flattery a get you nowhere" she said, smiling. "May I have a Mimosa?" she ordered when the bartender returned with Thug's bottle.

"I didn't think it would, that's why I've never used it" Thug charmed, getting close to her. Honesty has always been my weapon of choice" he told her.

Keys took a deep breath. She got a whiff of Paco Rabanne Gold. His masculine scent mesmerized her. There was something about Thug that she couldn't quite put her finger on. No man had ever made her feel like that. Not since she met her daughter's father. Thug's presence made her wet.

"By da way, my friends call me Thug" he introduced himself, sticking out his hand.

"Nice to meet you" she shook his hand. "But why Thug?"

"Long story. Maybe I'll fill you in some other time" he said. "But believe me when I say, I'm as roughish thuggish as da name suggests" he teased.

Keys smiled. "I'm from da show me state" she teased him back.

"What if I showed you how much I wanted to kiss those pretty lips of yours...?" he offered.

"I'd say what's stoppin' you?" she flirted.

Thug placed his drink on the bar leaned in and kissed her. Demon made a choking sound in his throat to get her attention.

"They waitin' for you on da stage" Demon said, eyeing Thug when they broke away from their kiss.

"Okay, um..." Keys stalled, wiping her lips with the back of her hand. "This is Demon. My handy man. Demon, meet Thug" she introduced the two.

"What up?" Thug nodded coyly. "Why don't you give me your number so I can call and we can discuss bizness?"

"Yeah, hold on" Keys dug in her purse to retrieve her phone. "Why don't you give me yours? And I'll give you a ring" she said.

"Cool" Thug gave her his number. "Maybe we can become friends, and I can fill you in on why they call me Thug" he told her.

"She don't need no new friends" Demon growled, grabbing her by the arm like a watchdog. "I'm all da friends she needs" he snapped as he pulled her away.

Thug watched her leave. She looked back over her shoulder to admire him, and Thug smiled. His grandmother always told him that, if a woman looked back, you had a chance. He knew they would become acquainted real soon.

* * * * *

Tooley stood incognito in the shadows. He watched Keys' every move waiting for her to make a mistake. He knew she would. And when she did, he would drop her like a bad habit.

* * * * *

Thug made his way to the VIP section. Keys made her way to the stage.

"Wuz up, lover boy?" Snake joked as he took a seat next to him in the booth. "I see you were over there bein' da lyfe of da party"

Thug laughed and glanced around the club to see where the rest of his cronies were before answering. Trouble and Roc'star was grooving with a couple of broads. Toe Tag was in the corner rapping to Cookie. Gunna was nowhere to be found.

"Yea, somethin' you should be doin' instead of cooped up in this booth" he shot back. "You seen Diamond? She should have been here by now" he said.

"Nah, I ain't seen her" Snake replied, eyeing the dancefloor. Something had caught his eye. "But I'm about to go take your advice and mingle. Excuse me" said Snake as he slid out the booth.

Thug checked his phone. He found it strange for Diamond not to be around. She had just texted him, and said she was on the way. Thug sent a text back and laid back and let the drink take effect.

* * * * *

"Glad to see all da faces that came out tonight in support of me and my late daughter, Candy" Keys spoke into the mic, and the crowd went wild. "Is everyone enjoyin' my Black Panther theme?" she asked amid more cheering.

"I really wish my daughter was here to see this" she continued. "She'd be just as excited as you are. Though she isn't here in person, I know she is here in-" Keys froze mid-sentence and the microphone slipped from her hand. Tooley's face lingered in the crowd. Chills ran down her spine. She closed her eyes a moment and took a deep breath. When she opened them, he was gone. She thought he might have been a hallucination. As soon as she bent down to retrieve the mic, twelve swarmed the place. Everyone started to scatter, and Benson rushed onto the stage.

"I have a warrant for your arrest" he informed, slapping the cuffs on her. "You have the right to remain silent. Anything you say can be used against you in the court of law. You have the right to an attorney, if you can't afford one, one will be appointed to you" he told her.

Keys laughed as she was escorted out the club. She had heard it all before. This wasn't the first time he'd arrested her. To think she would talk or could afford an attorney, made the matter hysterical. She would be out in the matter of hours.

Chapter Nine

* * * * *

The heat was sweltering. The sun beamed down blistering as Toe Tag rolled through Milwaukee streets. He put up his visor to block it from beating down on him. He and Snake rolled through the North side squalor. All the hood rats and gold diggers were out and about. They hadn't let the heat put a damper on their hustle.

Toe Tag's phone rang. He passed Snake the blunt he was smoking on and answered.

"Yo" he said.

"Last chance" Smuv warned. "This your last chance to reconsider and bring me my ice b'fo shit get real ugly" he threatened.

"Fuck yo bitch ass!" Toe Tag shouted. Snake gave Toe Tag a look.

"I told cha ain't no peace treat with da ops" Toe Tag retorted. "You hear what da fuck I'm sayin', pussy?"

"Loud and clear" Smuv replied, then the line went dead.

Toe Tag tossed the phone on the dashboard.

"What was that all about?" Snake inquired, taking the last pull of the Exotic before placing the roach on the ashtray.

"We gon have ta trump that bitch nigga, Smuv" Toe Tag answered.

"We should've done that shit at first" Snake replied.

"Bitch ass nigga keep callin' my phone hasslin' me with them idle threats" Toe Tag fumed.

"My nigga, on da streets, ain't no such thing as idle threats." Snake said. He worried about the matter. They not only had to look over they back, Toe Tag's brother might have to watch his ass too. "Niggaz out here play for keeps. You should tell yo brotha what 'cha did, so he can be on da lookout. Just in case buddy on something for real" he offered.

"Hell nah, fuck that nigga. That bitch ain't on shit" Toe Tag spat and got out the car.

Gunna was on the sidewalk serving a fiend when they walked up. The devotee tossed the stones in his mouth, so he could swallow if twelve came, and treaded up the block.

"Wuz up, Bananas n' Pajamas?" Snake cracked on the twins.

"Shit, what up with you, playa?" Gunna asked stepping back on the porch. "And Toe Tag" she added flatly, shooting a sly jab at him.

"Shawty" he returned with a deviant smile.

"Ay, what I tell you about that shawty shit?" Gunna jumped to her feet. "You just gon keep callin' me that shit until I hit 'cha in da mouth?"

"Please" Tags waved her off. "You think I'm worried about some four-foot-two midget?" he laughed.

Gunna wasn't laughing. She was fuming with loathsome rage. She was so mad, she was shaken. Swiftly, she pulled her gun out from her waist.

"What 'cha gon do, shoot me now?" he asked.

"Nah, Imma gold finger your ass" she said. "Here, hold my piece, bro" she handed Roc'star her Toz revolver. Gunna leaped from the porch and threw a blow. She put her might into it, but Toe Tag dodged it, stepping to the side. He was still laughing. His actions only enraged her more. She swung more wildly. With every swing, Tag dodged.

"Bring your bitch ass on and fight me like a man!" she huffed. "Yo bitch ass always talkin' all that gee shit. Then when it get gangsta, you duckin' and dodgin'!"

"Y'all chill with that mess" Snake intervened, swooping Gunna up from behind and holding her.

"Let me da fuck go!" she struggled to free herself from his grasp.

"Alright, but you betta go sit da fuck down. Or me and you gon have a misunderstandin'" he threatened, letting her go.

She eyed Toe Tag, eyes like piercing darts. But she didn't charge. Instead, she grabbed her gun from her brother and took a seat. Snake had a lot of pull, especially when it came to the promise of fighting. No one in the hood had hands like him. They witnessed him on numerous occasions knock niggas out. He was swift and fast. So fast he would hit you ten to twenty times before you even knew what hit you.

"Y'all two need to chill with that bullshit" Snake warned.

"That be him" she pointed out. "He always talkin' all dat rah rah shit" she ranted.

"It don't even matter who did what. All I'm sayin' is squash da shenanigans. I mean that shit" Snake said, putting his foot down.

* * * * *

Thug sat up in bed and yawned. Wiping the crust from his eyes, he looked over his shoulder at Faye's side of the bed. She was nowhere in sight. The faint aroma of fried eggs and bacon hit his nose. Thug got up and used the bathroom and exfoliated before heading downstairs.

"Good morning, sleepy head." she said, smiling over her shoulder when he entered the kitchen. She was cooking in nothing but his t-shirt. "You sleep like a log, I thought you'd never wake up" she told him.

Thug crept up behind her and wrapped his arms about her waist. He kissed her neck and she turned and kissed him on the mouth.

"That's from all da hard work I put in last night" Thug's hand slid beneath the shirt and palmed her bare butt. She gave a moan of satisfaction, as his hand ventured around and played with her moist twat.

"Don't worry I prepared a feast so you can get your strength back up" she purred.

Faye turned back around to slide the eggs from the Copperhead skillet. There was eggs, bacon, toast, and pancakes on the counter. She fixed him a plate and placed it in front of him. With a cup of Welch's grape juice.

"Eat up" she directed, sounding motherly.

"Da only thing I have a taste for is you" Thug said, pushing the plate away and pulling Faye onto his lap. "I was dreamin' about you" he murmured in between kisses.

"I can see…" she laughed pointing to his crotch. He stood tall like a flagpole. "I have to talk to you about something" she told him.

"You standin' in a corn field, I'm all ears" he replied.

"How would you feel about havin' kids?" she asked.

"I don't know…" he answered seriously. "I honestly never gave it any thought" he admitted.

"Well, do you have da time now?" she pressed on.

Thug got the gist. He wasn't slow by a long shot. He grabbed her tightly in his arms and hugged her to show his support. "No wonder that thang was so wet last night" he said.

"So is that your way of sayin you're happy?" she asked him.

"You know that!" he enthused.

Faye got so excited that she almost tumbled them both from the chair. She hugged him back and planted kisses all over his face, neck, and chest.

"Oh, God, we're gonna be parents!" she exclaimed. "I'm so happy you approve. I was so scared you wouldn't be happy for us" she continued.

"How far along are you?" Thug placed his hand on her stomach. "You still got that Britney Spears' washboard stomach" he commented.

"Forget you, you callin' me white?" she joked, popping him lightly on the head.

"You said that, not me" he said, teasing her.

"I'm not sure though, I peed on a home pregnancy test and it came back positive, after I kept experiencing mornin' sickness. I haven't been able to keep most of my food down…" she continued.

"That's probably your food runnin' away from your ugly self" he joked as Faye swatted Thug on the arm.

"Shut up, stupid" she giggled. "I'm bein' serious right now!"

""Okay, I'm sorry…" he apologized and kissed her. "Why don't you call and set up a doctor's appointment so I can make sure my son is okay?"

"What makes you so sure it's a boy?" she asked, feeling surprised.

"Because you got wide hips" he joked, and she swatted him again. "Nah, but serious though. Set up a doctor's appointment. I don't want my child comin' out with no football head like Stewie off Family Guy" he said.

"You mean like your head?" she joked this time.

"Hardy, ha, ha" Thug mocked. "You got jokes huh?"

Thug's phone rang and he answered. It was Trouble calling to tell him he was out front.

"Look, bae, Imma bout to dip out with da guys" Thug ran and got dressed. "I'll see you later beautiful" he said kissing her on the lips.

"Be careful, beau" she said.

"Always" he replied as pulled his .45 Smith & Wesson from his pocket and cocked it, then placed it back.

"I never leave home without it" he assured, kissing Faye one last time before he left.

* * * * *

Smuv distanced himself back behind three cars. He trailed in
pursuit of Rat Tahoe. Vulture rode the shotgun, and they
both was oblivious to anyone on their tail...

* * * * *

"Grab that box of pampers and bag of clothes for me, will
you?" Rat asked grabbing his son from the car seat and
putting the diaper bag over his shoulder. "Gotta keep da lil
man fresh. This bitch ain't gon do it. She too busy bar
hoppin'. Makin' sure this other nigga son fresh to death, like
she only got one child. I tell you, dawg, that favoritism shit
really gets under my skin. So, despite of it all, I make sure da
lil one don't need for nothin'" he complained, ringing the
doorbell. "Ain't that right, lil man?" he asked Jermaine who
was between him and the door.

Tasha opened the door in a pair of boy shorts and Victoria
Secret's sports bra. Her hair was wrapped up in a towel, and
it appeared she'd just gotten out the shower.

"What I tell you about comin' to da damn door in your
underwear?" Rat snapped at her.

"Boy, please..." Tasha sucked her teeth and rolled her eyes.
"You act as if Vulture somebody" she took her son into her
arms. "Plus, I just got out the shower" she responded.

Tasha wasn't a bad looking girl. Rat wasn't intimidated by her beauty. It just really pissed him off when she flaunted her body freely. He felt as if she wasn't setting a good example for their son.

"Your ass still should've put some damn clothes on before opening da door!" Rat snapped in frustration. His yelling startled little Jermaine, who began to cry.

"Look what you did!" she berated, mugging Rat. "It's okay baby, your daddy just being stupid" she cooed rocking the boy on her hip to soothe him.

A bullet whizzed right by Rat's head and ricocheted off the mailbox. The trajectory of the bullet bounced off and grazed Tasha across the right cheek. She dropped to the floor screaming, cradling their screaming son in a fetal position. Rapid bullets flew their way. Rat dived in the house to protect his son and Tasha. He was pulling his gun and leaning against the foyer wall as more bullets clanked against the porch of the home. It was pandemonium. Screams and gunshots engulfed him. Vulture dived over the railing and landed flat on his belly. He crawled on his stomach until he was safely behind a tree. He stood and peeked beyond it to see if he could see the shooter. Tree barks flew off as he stuck his head around. He couldn't see the shooter, so he had no way to know where his vantage point was. Vulture had left his strap in the truck. So, he made a hasty run for it. Fleeing toward the truck, he caught a slug in the side, and tumbled and fell on his back. He lied there gazing into the sky. Trying to catch his breath, his lungs began to give way and he gurgled up blood. As he fought for breath, a strange figure loomed over him.

"Smuv!" Vulture breathed.

"Nah, da reaper" He said and squeezed the trigger, emptying the remainder of the 32-shot extension on the Glock 9 into him.

* * * * *

"This shit you pigs pullin' a clear violation of my Miranda rights!" Keys shouted. Her voice echoed throughout the small cubical interrogation room. "I've been held ova 72 hours and I want my attorney!" she ranted. She was so infuriated, her skin was red.

Benson and Brown shared a laugh at Keys' expense. She sucked her teeth.

"If you cherish time, all you have to do is tell us where Hernandez Mendez is" Benson requested. "We know he was involved in the Parker and Jones family murders. Just like we know you made the call" he said.

"How many times I gotta tell you two pork chops I don't speak pig Latin. Do I look like Master Splinter?" Keys huffed. "For da last time, I don't know no muthafuckin' Mendez" she fumed. "You know what happen da last time y'all two pigs' feet arrested me on conspiracy to commit murder, right?" Keys leaned forward in her chair. "I was released in a matter of hours. Just like I'll be out of here soon" she snapped.

"You really believe that don't you?" Benson stood and strode around the table. He squatted next to Keys. "That won't be the case today. We have you this time, Keys. So, you might as well tell us what we want to know to save yourself. I'm not the smartest man in the world-"

"You can say dat again" Keys scoffed.

"I know Mendez is your henchmen" Benson finished. He was hoping his words carried some type of shock value. His CI had told him Hernandez 'Hurk' Mendez was there. And he could bet his bottom dollar, Keys right-hand man, Demon, or some other of her goons had executed that family, at her request.

"My, you two little piggies sure is stupid" Keys said.

"That's it, you common criminal. We are tired of playing games with you. Either you tell us what we want to hear, or you'll rot in here" Brown leaped from his chair shouting and pointing his finger when Keys' attorney barged in.

"You're in here spreading propaganda again" Tracy Woods said. "My client won't be a worm on you guys' fishing expedition" she said.

"You can't come in here like that. Get out!" Benson demanded. "Who do you think you are?"

"You cops really don't know when you're in over your heads..." Woods spoke calmly, shaking her head at the buffoons before her. "As to who I am... I'm the one who will be reporting you to the chief commissioner for unlawfully interrogating my client without due process rights, if you don't let her walk right this second" Woods threatened. "And you two will be walking the beat, directing traffic cones the rest of career" Woods seethed, inching closer to Benson and Brown.

"Well, it was nice watchin' you guys play good cop. bad cop" Keys mocked rising for her seat. "And by da way, Mr. Brown. I'm more than a common criminal. I'm a master mind" she said, walking out the door behind her lawyer.

Benson and Brown stood quietly. They were both tired of Keys getting off the hook so easily. It seemed that Lady Justice was on her side and they were just buying time. Sooner or later, Benson would get her. And when he did, Keys would rot in a jail cell for the rest of her life.

Chapter Ten

* * * * *

T hug rushed into St. Joseph's hospital emergency room.

"What up?" Thug asked. The whole team was there waiting, lodging in the chairs. "I got y'all urgent 911 text. It ain't Trouble, is it?" He really hoped it wasn't Trouble. Trouble only came to mind because he was present, and he was always in the middle of something.

"Nah, it's Vulture" Snake sobered.

In a way, Thug found the news refreshing. It wasn't one of his cronies and that made the burden less stressful. He had been enjoying a matinee with Faye before getting that text.

"What happened?" he pressed on. "He ain't dead, is he?"

"Nah, that nigga Smuv." Snake replied, lowering his head. "That nigga popped Vulture tryna get back at me and Tags" he explained.

"Damn, that's serious…" Thug replied.

"What's goin' on?" Faye asked, rushing in. She had let Thug come in first while she searched for a parking spot.

"Snake a fill you in" Thug informed her. "Imma go holla at Tags and see how he holdin' up" he kissed Faye, then headed over to Toe Tag. As he approached Tags, the doctor strode up.

"John" Thug gasped. "What da fuck? Since when have you been a doctor?"

"Since always" John replied. "You never asked" he pointed out.

Thug couldn't argue with that. He never asked John about his profession. With his suspicions about Trouble being twelve and him serving John, he never thought to ask.

"By the way, keep the fact you know me under your hat" John requested. "I have a lot on the line. And I can't afford a scandal that involves me with drugs. You understand, right?"

"Your secret's safe with us" Thug said.

"You the next of kin?" John asked Toe Tag, looking up from his clipboard.

"Yeah" Tags confirmed. "We all we got too, doc" he added. "Our parents been dead ever since I was eleven and he was fifteen. So, don't let my brother die" he pleaded.

"Sorry to hear that" John sympathized. "Your brother pulled through the surgery. It wasn't easy. He lost a lot of blood, and one of his lungs collapsed-"

"So, will he make it?" Toe Tag interrupted.

"That's still hard to determine. He is still in the ICU, and I can't make a proper prognosis. He was shot ten times, his lung collapsed, and his viscera ruptured. The only thing we can do is play it by ear. Time will tell" John said.

"Can I see him?" Tags asked.

"I don't know if that is such a good idea. He needs to rest" John advised.

"Come on. I need to see him." Tags begged.

John looked down a moment. Thug could see he was considering.

"Okay, but it will only be a moment. And I'll only allow one of you in" John told Tags, who was relieved.

* * * * *

Diamond was brought back to consciousness by a splash of water to the face. She had vomited all over herself and she reeked.

"I'm gonna give you one last chance to answer me truthfully" Bullet proposed. "If you don't, I'm gonna start by shooting your kneecaps off, and then your ankles. By da time I'm done you'll beg to tell me what I want to know" he threatened.

Diamond was petrified, divested and zip tied to an old rocking chair in the middle of the basement floor. She didn't even remember how she'd gotten there. All she knew she was battered and bruised.

"Dawg, I'm hungry..." Parlay spoke. It was off-kilter and peculiar his request for food at a time like now. "Imma go order some Grub Hub" he said.

"Alright, I'm kinda hungry myself" Bullet confirmed.

Parlay went upstairs, leaving Bullet in the basement with Diamond.

"Now, what will it be?" he asked as soon as Parlay was out of sight.

Diamond sat there motionless staring at the chrome gun aimed at her kneecap. Paralyzing fear compelled her to weigh her options. Before, she would have never considered any other possibility, other than death. But now she wondered if he was worth dying for. Ever since he started fucking Faye, she had been playing second fiddle to none. Diamond didn't have a problem with Thug fucking other women. They had an open relationship, and she was open-minded. But what she couldn't stand was him being in love with another female. Ever since Faye had come into the picture, that seemed to be the case. He no longer showed Diamond the admiration and affection he once had. She either choose love and die or live for herself.

"What do you want to know...?" she cried.

* * * * *

Trouble entered G's Clipper's and sat in his favorite barber's chair.

"What up?" Tone greeted, shaking Trouble's hand. "It seems like light years since a nigga last seen you" he started small talk.

"You do know light years measure distance, not time, right?" Trouble asked.

"Suppose you're right..." Tone replied.

"I know I'm right." Trouble quipped. They both laughed.

"But where you been?" Tone asked.

"I been grindin', and I ain't really had time to focus on myself" he explained.

"Shit, it shows" Tone replied, handing Trouble a mirror. "It look like u ain't shaved in months. You come up in here with 'cha beard lookin' like you in trainin' to be Freeway!"

I know... I know" Trouble acknowledged, laughing. "It don't seem like you missed me too much" Trouble pointed around to the customers the filled the barbershop and patted Tone's pocket. "Your pockets still fat" he said.

"I can't complain, I do well" Tone fastened the barber smock around Trouble. "Da more money, more problems" he added.

"Then give me da problems!" Trouble retorted. "I got problems without it. So maybe with it I can withstand da test of time a little better. Money always been da root to every black person problems anyways" he mused.

"Money also the root of all evil" Tone said.

They caught up on old times. When Tone was done cutting, he passed Trouble the mirror. Trouble paid forty for his haircut and tipped Tone a twenty. He was on his way out the door when he overheard someone sneak dissing his man.

"I can't even begin to explain how me and that bitch ass nigga Thug is related. We as different as night and day" the person said.

The words caused Trouble to stop in his tracks and hone in on the conversion.

"I can't believe my mom's that nigga auntie. But I sho whooped dat nigga ass like we weren't family" Champ and his barber laughed, shaking hands.

"What Thug you talkin' about?" Trouble confronted him. "You better not be talkin' bout my main man off da trays."

"What if I am?" Champ challenged, snatching his smock off his neck.

Trouble didn't even give him a chance to stand to his feet. As soon as the smock came off, Trouble knocked him off the stool. He fell, knocking over the barber's appliances and cosmetics. Tone rushed to the commotion and grabbed

Trouble from behind. That was a mistake. Trouble pulled his .9mm from his pocket and placed it at Tone's side.

"Let me da fuck go, b'fo I turn your insides to mush" he hissed.

Tone backed off and Trouble crotched down and beat Champ about the head.

"Nigga, empty out your pockets!" he ordered, turning Champ's pockets inside out. What was inside infuriated him. Champ had a hundred-dollar bill and a pack of cigarettes.

"You and my bitch ass cousin better hope I don't catch you slippin'." Champ threatened. Too much had happened lately for him to take the threat lightly.

"Don't worry. Da only way u'll see us again is in hell." Trouble retorted and pulled the trigger. Champ lied down riddled, three to the chest and two to the head.

Trouble turned to flee, then found himself surrounded.

"Drop your weapon and get on the ground!" one of the officers ordered through the megaphone.

Trouble thought of going out in a blaze of glory. Holding court on the street instead of street in court. Weighing the options, Trouble decided he had too much to live for. So, he dropped the gun and got down on the ground.

* * * * *

Keys attacked Demon as soon as he opened the front door to enter his humble abode. She pushed him up against the wall, pawing at his bare muscular chest as she kissed him desperately.

"I missed you…" she cooed. "Why didn't you come over as soon as I got out? I expected to see you there" she told him.

Demon pushed Keys away and walked into the bedroom. Keys followed close behind.

"Because you wasn't too happy to see me when ole boy had his tongue down your throat da other night. That's why" he huffed flopping down on the bed. "And quite frankly, I don't know how I feel about it. So, I gave you some space" he said.

"You illin' beau." Keys said, sitting next to Demon on the bed and hugging him. "You need to stop trippin'. You know me and you tight. Me, you, and Cam'ron are a team" she replied.

"It didn't look like no teamwork when buddy was workin' on you" she snapped, jealousy dripping down every word.

"You wiggin' out. You know damn well I'm just playin' da game. Ole boy you jealous of might be da one to handle da little problem" she offered.

"What little problem?" Demon asked.

"Tooley out" she spat.

Demon scoffed. Here he was thinking the past was way behind him, and it was only catching up. Tooley was a bad ghost from the past. One him and Keys had did dirty. If he was out, he knew they had bigger problems than they could fathom. Demon knew Tooley would be gunning for the throne.

"That ain't no problem I can't handle." Demon replied unconcerned. "You know I'm handy with da tool" he said.

"Don't worry about it. I already got somethin' up my sleeve that doesn't require your handy with da tool skills. It'll be like killin' two birds with one stone" she replied.

"All I'm sayin' is you didn't have to stick your tongue down some nigga throat to get it done when you got me" Demon scoffed.

"We still on that, beau?" Keys asked annoyed. It was so unattractive. "Let me see if I can draw you out your funk" she soothed him. Keys kissed Demon, pulling his swizzle from his shorts. She took his flaccid dick in her mouth and sucked him long and hard until he rocked up. He moaned locking his fingers in her hair.

"Nuh uh" she said, taking him from her mouth, and slapping his hand away. "Keep your hands to yourself or I'm done" she said, then took him back into her slobbering mouth. Keys liked to be in control. She was the apex, the top species of all beings. She didn't like having anyone having power over her. Keys released Demon from her mouth again, pulled her dress up to her waist, then straddled him. She slowly descended on him, enjoying every pleasurable moment of him penetrating her. It had been four days and it felt good to be filled. Keys began to ride him. All Demon could do was lay back and moan and groan.

"Ah, Keys..." he breathed as she rode him like a mechanical bull. Her manicured nails dug deep into his chest. She rode him wildly, his eleven inches sliding in and out of her with ease. Demon knew she was about to cum because her thrusts became more urgent. Keys stiffened and came hard.

"Yes, God, yes..." she moaned.

When she was done, she lifted herself off of Demon and smoothed her dress back down.

"W-what are u doin'?" he asked confused as she stood in the bedroom mirror fixing her hair.

"I got mine, now you have to get yours..." she answered, cold. Demon looked puzzled.

"I know you ain't gon leave me like this, Keys, come on..." he begged grabbing his hard joint. "At least let me get mine" he insisted.

"Maybe that'll teach you to stop actin' like a lil bitch" she barbed, walking towards the door. "And, I know where that bitch Krazy is hidin'. I need you to assemble a team and involve Ecstasy. I want her to pull the trigger. I'll text you da address when you're ready" she said and walked out the door, leaving Demon with a hard dick and full of frustration.

Chapter Eleven

* * * * *

T hug jumped awake, startled by his phone vibrating on his lap. He yawned and wiped his sweaty face.

"Hello..." he answered, only to hear an automated reply. It was his boy, Trouble, calling collect from Milwaukee County Jail. He pressed five to answer.

"Tell me your wild ass ain't really locked up?" Thug asked in disbelief.

"I wished that was da case. But da reality of da matter, I'm locked up and they won't let me out" Trouble spoke somberly, disappointed in himself. "I then got myself in some deep shit this time, and I need your help. I can't call Jackie, 'cause I don't want her directly connected to this. So, when you get a chance, call her and tell her Imma get at her, but I gotta make sure she stay in da shadows if you know what I mean..." he elaborated.

"Fam, it sound like you got yourself fuckin deeper than da Grand Canyon. Tell me what 'cha did now, fam?"

Trouble didn't even know where to begin. The gravity of the situation weighed heavily. How could he tell Thug what he had done? What he had to say could tarnish their friendship forever. It wasn't like he could hide what he did. So, he knew the best thing was to do was tell the truth.

"I trumped Champ!" he blurted out. "Dawg, don't be mad. It all happened so fast, and I had to do it" Trouble wailed.

"You did what?" Thug couldn't believe his ears. "What da fuck, my nigga? What da fuck am I supposed to tell my auntie? I mean… how am I supposed to tell her one of my closest dogs trumped her only son?" he said, flustered. He was stuck between a rock and a hard place. There was no way he could possibly explain his dilemma to his aunt. This was a serious matter and he needed time to think.

"Look, dawg, Imma call Jackie for you, but you gon have to hit me back later. It's some serious shit goin' down up here at da hospital. We was lookin' for your ass last night, and your ass is locked up" Thug said.

"Why, what happened?" Trouble asked.

"Call me back later, and I'll holler at you then" Thug hung up and stormed out of the hospital.

* * * * *

Main ran his fingernail down the compressed wrapped brick and hit a bump.

"Damn, that's that butta right there…" Main confessed sniffling and flicking the tip of his numbed nose. "This shit better than your last batch. When you get some fish scale like this?"

Krazy's phone pinged with an incoming text. He checked the display. The text was from an unknown number, and they'd left a threat. A water gun, boy running, smiling face devil. Krazy frowned and chalked it up as a wrong contact.

"Boy, that coke must got you delusional" Krazy quipped. "I always got A1. Wings of a butterfly, my nigga" he continued.

Main handed Krazy a tower of hundreds.

"That twenty-five gees right there. You can count it if you want" Main said.

"I trust you" Krazy took the money and stuffed it in his book bag. "I'll get next week. Same place, same time?" Krazy asked, trying to establish a set date.

"I don't know, I'll call you. You know I gotta keep movin' cause that bitch Keys got eyes on me" Main warned.

"Already" Krazy observed.

They gave each other dap, then Main departed. Krazy stepped out right after him. Hopping in his truck, he pulled into traffic. Going nowhere in particular, he just wanted to get out. He was tired of being cooped up. He pulled to the stop light on Hopkins & Burleigh, across from the cemetery. A gray Rav 4 came to a halt next to him. Krazy turned, and he almost shit bricks from what he saw. Demon was in the passenger seat and Ecstasy was in the back with a Corbind 1 aimed out the window. She pulled the trigger and the first shot missed. The bullet shattered his front windshield, and he hit the gas. Almost wrecking someone else car by a head-on collision, he swerved around the SUV, but Demon and Ex were right on his tail as he zoomed through traffic.

Ecstasy raised the rifle to fire a second time, but the magazine popped out. She scrambled on the back floor of the speeding vehicle to retrieve it. When she did, she stuffed it back in a let off a chain of rounds. The slug blew out his back window as they came to a sharp turn on 27th & Burleigh. Krazy's truck collided with a UPS truck, and wrapped him around a traffic light pole. The airbags deployed and he struggled desperately to free himself from the confines of the truck. Hurk pulled beside him and Ecstasy leveled the high-powered rifle again and fired. The bullet ripped through his torso as he dived for the back seat. He struggled with the door.

"Help!" he shouted to onlookers and pedestrians who stared on in horror. "Somebody call da police. They tryin' to kill me!"

Ecstasy fired rapidly. The bullets ripped through Krazy's body like toilet tissue. One bullet entered the back of his head and came out his face, blowing his nose out the side window onto the bus stop. Hurk hit the gas and the tires squealed. The trio sped away up Burleigh.

* * * * *

Thug rushed into Omega's diner and took a swift seat across from Keys.

"I see you're not fond of keepin prompt schedules..." said Keys, leaning forward in her seat in a flirtatious manner.

Keys was dressed sexy, but still elegant in Givenchy apparel. It showed a lot of clavicle and tasteful cleavage.

"I wasn't gon come..." Thug confessed. "A lot of shit been goin' on lately. But when you called, I figured it'll be rude to leave you seatin' and waitin'" he said.

Keys set her menu down on the table and stared Thug in the eye. She found his brutal honesty refreshing.

"You want to talk about it?" She asked with sincere concern.

"Nah, I'd rather get right to da point. It'll pass" he reassured her.

"A true biznessman. That's ' what I like" she praised him.

"Here's your menu, sir. I'll be you waiter today" a young waiter lingered over their table, placing the menu down. "May I get you a beverage, sir?"

Keys had already ordered while she waited for Thug to arrive.

"A water" Thug ordered.

"Okay, I'll be right back" the waiter said.

"I would like to know what took you so long to get at me, though?" he resumed, going off-topic, as soon as the waiter was gone. "What, your man had you under lock and key?"

"Who, Demon?" Keys answered, laughing at how naive men could be. "Don't you know I'm a boss? I don't have time for men. I have D-boyz" she confessed.

"Well, he certainly didn't seem like no D-boy. Da way buddy was actin', snatchin' you by your arm and shit. He certainly had me fooled. I would've thought he was your man" Thug replied.

"Well, looks can be deceivin' now, can't they?" she said. "I'm still lookin' for a real man to tame me..." Keys winked.

"Sometimes you ain't gotta look that far. Why search over da horizon for flowers that bloom right under your windowsill?" he asked her. Keys pondered on Thug words a moment.

"Is that so?" she replied.

"Seek and you shall find" he said.

"All in good time..." she promised, covering his hand with hers. "Let's talk about what I called you here for today" she continued.

"Here's your water" the waiter returned, placing the beverage on the table, then pulled out his pad and a pen. "Are you two ready to order?"

Thug ordered the lasagna, and Keys the Fraser salad.

"Okay, coming right up" the waiter replied and took their menus, then headed off to the kitchen.

"I did my homework on you, Thug. And I must say I'm impressed by your résumé…" Keys said. "It seems you have a trap house not too far from us. Is that so?"

"Yeah, but what does that have to do with why I'm here?" Thug asked.

It was true, Thug had a trap on 36th & Galena. Not too far from Keys.

"Don't worry, that's not why we are here today" she reassured him. "I hear you have quite a name on da streets, and you are very rapacious. I need someone like you on my team. I think with you, da possibilities will be unlimited" Keys offered.

"Yeah, and what about your lap dog?" Thug asked, referring to Demon.

"Let me tell you about any misunderstandings you may have about me… Imma boss, and don't nobody run shit around. I call da shots and make my own rules." she spoke. "I'm offerin' you a deal of a lifetime. And want you to take it. I can promise you'll be a millionaire by da end of da year. Leave da remedy to Demon to me" she said, her voice firm.

Thug took in her words, rubbing his right earlobe. It was something he did to think.

"I'll take it under one condition" he proposed after great consideration. The promise of becoming a millionaire was too alluring. "My family eat with me. I won't leave them behind. We come together; we eat together" he concluded.

"I'll have it no other way" she replied, smiling. "How does a honeybun upfront and five thangs a month sound?"

"I'll say that's settled" Thug replied.

"My word is my bond" Keys shook Thug's hand. "Why don't we skip lunch so you can fill me in on that story of how you got da name Thug?" she flirted, rising from her seat and taking Thug by the hand. "I've been dyin' to hear da story ever since da night at da club" she pulled him along, and they headed out the door together.

* * * * *

Benson was sitting at his desk, in the confines of his cramped office idly swiping his tablet when his partner entered the room carrying a suspicious package.

"This came for you" Brown said, setting the box on the desk.

"What is it?" Benson inquired.

"I don't know" Brown shrugged. "It just arrived, first class mail" he said.

Benson set his tablet on the table and picked the box up. It was heavy. He shook it, and something thumped on the inside.

"You think it's a bomb?" Brown asked.

"No" Benson answered. "It would've never made it through post if that was the case. Not with our package sniffing K-9 dogs" he said. Benson ripped the box open. A .45-caliber attached to a note was inside. Benson read the note.

"Oh...my...God..." Benson gasped. "Do you know what this is?"

"It looks like a gun?" Brown sarcastically replied.

"Not just any gun. This is the gun that killed the Ms. Parker and Jones. And coincidentally, is going to put Tooley back behind bars. Because this is the gun that could've upheld his conviction. Because it was used in his murder case. Unfortunately, the police could never retrieve the gun..."

"How do you know his fingerprints are on that gun? It has to be seventeen points to prove so" Brown went on with the ballistics, as if Benson wasn't aware how many points it took to prove a fingerprint. "And by the gun turning up now, doesn't it make you suspicious?"

Benson nodded his head in agreement. It was odd that the gun had now mysteriously appeared, right after he arrested Keys on conspiracy to have the family murdered. He scratched his head. He was sure someone was planting evidence to mislead him.

"I mean, even if his fingerprints are on that gun... the Supreme Court overturned the case. And it would be double jeopardy now" Brown said.

"True" Benson confirmed. "We might not be able to convict in retrospect, but if we can prove he killed Ms. Parker and

Ms. Jones, he'll never see the light of day again" he said. Benson picked up the phone and called analysis to his office to take the gun and dust for fingerprints.

Chapter Twelve

Thug's phone rang and he rolled over and picked his jeans up off the floor. Taking the phone out his pocket, he answered.

"Good mornin', my king" Faye chimed with glee into the phone. "You didn't come home last night. Are you okay beau?"

"Yeah milady, I'm coolin'" Thug said. "I stayed at Snake's last night." He was lying.

"It's fine. I just wanted to tell you that my ultrasound is scheduled for this mornin'" she said.

Thug slapped his forehead. "Baby, I totally forgot..." he confessed. "I gotta take a rain check, though. 'Cause I got some bizness to handle myself this mornin'. Then I was gon go visit granny's grave and put some flowers on the site. It's her birthday, and I haven't visited her in quite a while" he explained.

"It's okay, baby. I'll just let you know da news tonight. Just as long as you promise to be present at da next appointment" she said.

"I promise" he replied.

Keys leaned over and took Thug's morning wood in her mouth.

"Aaah" he sighed.

"You alright, baby?" Faye asked.

"Yeah, I'm all good with da exception of a hangover from last night" he lied.

"Well, Imma bout to get ready for my appointment. I'll see you later, baby. I love you" she told him.

"I luv you, too" he said.

Hanging up, he tangled his finger in Keys' hair.

* * * * *

"Remember, this is my operation" Benson stipulated to the commander and all the other police office's that were there for the raid. He stood toe to toe with the SWAT team commander. "I don't want any of your men to move, shoot, not even fart without my command. Do I make myself clear?"

"You got it" Commander Franklin agreed, throwing his arms in the air. They'd been quarreling over the matter, and he had grown tired of Benson's power trip. "It's your world. I'm just a squirrel trying to get a nut" he said.

"Alright, then on my call" Benson informed, squatting down beside the house with his service pistol drawn. "One, two, three... Go... Go.... Go!" he commanded.

* * * * *

Tooley dove from his bed. When the explosive breach blew the hinges off the front door. He grabbed the .50 caliber from under his pillow.

"Jammy, Keke!" Crystal set up screaming for their children.

"Get on da floor!" Tooley demanded, tugging her off the bed beside him. "I'll get da kids, don't worry. Just be still and quiet" he said as he crouched down in nothing but his boxers and crept out the dark room into the hallway.

"Daddy..." The twins called as he entered their room. He rushed to his weeping kids' side and took them into his arms. "Wuz goin' on dad?" Jammy asked.

"I don't know..." Tooley replied.

Tooley was clueless. He had no idea to what was going on. He snuck the children safely to his room. The twins rushed into their mother's arms.

"It's alright, babies..." she consoled, stroking their heads. They were shivering. "Everything is gonna be okay now. Momma got you..." she brought them closer to her.

Tooley crept back into the hall. Leaning against the wall, he could hear footsteps filing up the stairs and bright lights flashing over the railing. Tooley was shadowed in the darkness. When the first invader came upstairs, waving his gun around, Tooley got low and fired his gun around the corner. He let three rounds off rapidly. Two of the bullets caught the officer in the abdomen, knocking him to the floor. Wood splinters struck Tooley in the eye as the officers opened fire. Their automatic rifles and shotguns blasted chunks off the wall. Tooley shielded his eyes, recoiling back behind the wall. He rubbed the flanks out of his eyes.

"Put your weapon down and step out with your hands up!" Benson shouted. "I repeat, come out with your hands up!"

"Come out with my hands up for what? I ain't did shit!" Tooley refused. "I ain't comin' out so I can be another dead black man!"

"We just want to talk" Benson said.

"Where I'm from, when people come with guns, they don't come to talk" Tooley replied.

"These are only for your protection. We're the police" Benson informed, sliding his badge across the ground. "Those are my credentials" he continued. The shield slid across the floor and hit the side of the wall with a crass thump. Tooley bent down to retrieve the badge and a sniper rifle bullet came through the window at the end of the hall. It tore through his lower back and came out his chest.

I told you not to move without my order! was the last thing Tooley heard before he faded out of consciousness.

* * * * *

Faye sat next to the window in a Subway booth. She took a healthy bite of her roast beef and avocado sandwich. She checked her call log, then she hit send on her phone.

"Hey, gurl!" Cookie shrilled loudly in excitement. "I haven't heard from you in a while. You know since-"

"Don't even say it" Faye interrupted. "There is no use to livin' in da past. Trudgin' up old demons. Let's call it water under da bridge" she said.

"I understand" Cookie conceded. "What 'cha been up to, though, gurl?"

"Nothin', just comin' from my doctor's appointment" she answered.

"For what? You okay?" Cookie's voice was strained with concern.

"Oh, I'm fine, gurl. I just came back from an ultrasound. Makin' sure da baby fine..." she explained.

"What? Shut up, gurl" Cookie enthused. "You and Thug havin' a baby? How far along are you?"

"Twelve weeks" Faye answered.

"Did you tell Thug yet?" Cookie asked.

"He knows. Imma tell him da sex later when he get home" she told her.

"Tell me. I wanna know" Cookie nudged.

"Nope" Faye replied. "Thug will be da first to know" she went on.

"Okay, be like that…" Cookie pouted.

"I will. We should get together this weekend, and I'll tell you then after I tell him" Faye offered.

"Will do" she agreed. "I can't wait!"

Faye emptied her trash, finished her orange soda, then headed to her car. Faye made a right on 35th heading up North. She stopped at 41st & North at the red light. She was waiting on the light to turn green, when a red STS rolled alongside of her. She shuddered in fear as a masked man jumped out the passenger set with a Bush Master 223. The man raised the gun and brought the butt down hard, shattering the driver's window.

"Help!" Faye shrieked as the man reached for her.

* * * * *

Thug placed a bouquet on his grandmother's grave. He touched the front of her tombstone as he silently prayed. It had been a while since he had talked to God, or his grandmother, for that matter. Things on the streets were hectic. The streets was blazing in Milwaukee. The mortality rate climbed from local organized crime violence. War had been declared right in the middle of our wholesome neighborhood where peace should linger amongst the people... but the slaves to the establishment failed to come to the realization that the government's corrupt system cursed the African Americans way before the conception of black-on-black crime. In the 1960s, below poverty neighborhoods were flooded with heroin; and not long after, in the 1980s, the crack cocaine epidemic ensued. A form a freebasing was introduced to the broken, struggling black communities. In addition, a vast shipment of firearms was provided in toll to the average black man possessing a chip on his shoulder. It was no different from when America secretly provided the Iranians assault rifles to kill off Iraqis in 1982.

Above it all, Thug remained the same. Things were starting to look up for him. It was like his grandmother had always told him, stay true to yourself, and God would provide. Thug knew this was a completely different entity, however. He was traveling down the wrong road for it to be God's blessing. There was no explanation to how he was doing so good. Quite frankly, he felt real streets didn't need one. He could only focus on getting it how he lived.

BONUS BOOK NEXT PAGE

Chapter One

* * * * *

The game of Texas Hold 'Em was a monthly get-together with the guys from the office. Jerome Jackson was on the winning streak tonight, and out of exasperation of winning only the minimal pot, he suggested a game of no limits with Mac Shaun. At stake is the largest pot ever presented at the table. Problem is… Jerome is short staked against Mac.

Jerome is dealt pocket of kings. Across, is four of hearts, king of clubs, and eight of hearts. Mac checks. Jerome bets a third of his stack. Mac calls it. On the turn, is the king of spades. Seeing that, Jerome's pulse quickens as he finds it hard to believe his luck. Feeling wise, he decides to slow play the hand and not give anything away. Mac checks again. Jerome stalls and peeks at his cards. He has four kings. Without a doubt, he bets another third of his stack. Mac, of course, calls it. On the river is a five of hearts. Once again, Mac checks.

Jerome looks across the table and holds Mac in a steady gaze trying to read his expression. He checked each round, waiting to see what Mac is going to do. He could have a possible flush, a straight, or nothing at all. This was one of Jerome's best hands, four cowboys. Neither a straight nor flush could beat that. He concluded Mac must be trying to bluff him. Jerome studied Mac, searching for any indication that would give anything away. Then it came. He noticed the way Mac rubbed the upper corner of his face down card in a faint scratching motion. As if trying to scrape something better. Mac Shaun was a formidable poker player. He won more than he lost; and hardly ever bluffed. But when he did, he had a dead giveaway where he tended to rub the corner of his cards. Jerome pushed the remainder of his stack in.

"I'm all in" Mac said with a slur. He was slightly inebriated from the constant shots of Remy.

The veneer of Mac's stone expression cracked and gave way to a smirk. "I call, and raise all in" he said, pushing five stacks of his chips in. Jerome's jaw dropped. "I-I ain't got anything to cover that" he stammered. His entire paycheck for the month was already in the pot. "Guess your gonna have to fold" Mac replied. Jerome thought Mac was a sneaky son of a bitch! That was his plan from the start, to raise more than Jerome could cover to win by capitulation. It was obvious Mac didn't have shit! Still, if he can't call, what other choice did he have? Jerome asked the other guys if one of them could cover him, but each declined. Jerome unfastened his gold presidential Rolex, an anniversary gift from his wife, Carman, and tossed it on the pile of chips. "That should be worth da cover. It's worth at least thirty grand."

"Nah, I'm straight on collateral goods. I'm cash on da table" Mac announced with a slight smirk.

"What da fuck, dawg! Come on Mac, you know I'm good for that march" Jerome seethed.

Mac leaned forward like a devil ready to make a deal. "I like bein' paid in full. After all, that's what we all agreed on.

Jerome knew he had Mac beat, but he just couldn't fund it. There had to be something to this. "What do you want, Mac?" Jerome asked.

"Gentlemen, if you'll excuse us for a moment, Jerome and I need to negotiate an off da table arrangement" Mac said, motioning for the other players to leave. Mac leaned back in his chair. "Bet Carman" he suggested.

"What?!" Jerome blurted out. Mac couldn't be serious. Jerome knew he could take him in a fist fight. Jerome was well-built, but he knew that wouldn't be wise. Mac was a stone-cold killer. It was a reason his hand was beneath the table. Jerome could beat his bottom dollar that it was on the trigger of his gun. "Bet your wife for da weekend?" Mac suggested, again.

Jerome was livid. "Are you fuckin' nuts? What da hell kind of deal is that?"

Mac cracked an arrogant smile. "It's a gamble. Gamblin' is based on risk. You believe you have da winning hand, but you must be willin' to take da risk" he said.

Jerome knew he had the better hand, but Mac was playing with the barrel of a gun. He was trying to intimidate him into folding. "You want me to bet my wife for da weekend?" Jerome thought Mac wasn't crazy enough to do it.

"Of course, I want you to bet your wife. Under certain conditions" Mac continued as if it was all a casual conversation. "She must be willin' to participate. If she refuses to comply, at any time durin' da weekend, da deal will be voided. I'll see to it you pay me my money, or I'll kill you. Let me even sweeten da deal, after da weekend is over, I'll even return your watch and money" he offered.

The sanctimonious bastard, Jerome thought. He knew Mac thought he had him by the balls. There was more than three times his paycheck on the table. More than enough to finally get out of debt... If he lost, that would be his entire month's salary. He needed to pay his bills. After Carman had been laid off, he was the only one with any income in their home. Okay" Jerome made up his mind. "I'll call" he said, tossing a pair of kings on the pile of chips. "Four kings, beat that!" Mac smirked while slowly flipping over his cards, revealing the six and seven of hearts. "Straight flush."

Blinking incredulously while swallowing a lump of trepidation, Jerome felt dread creeping under his skin. What was he going to tell Carman? He couldn't back out of the deal. Mac would kill him.

"I'll be expectin' Carman to arrive at my apartment by seven o'clock this Friday evenin', and have her wear somethin' nice. I'm goin' to take her out for a drink first" Mac announced from across the table.

* * * * *

"You what?" Carman snapped. She couldn't believe her ears, dwelling on what Jerome just told her. Standing in her pink Victoria's Secret nightgown, she confronted her husband. "You wagered me in a fuckin' poker game? What the hell would make you do such a thing?"

"I thought I would—should have won."

Carman's hazel eyes burned with fury. "I can't believe you bet me like I'm some kind of slut!" Jerome turned away from her scornful gaze. "I didn't bet you, Carman, it was Mac's suggestion."

"Oh" she uttered with sardonic pitch. "That's supposed to make it sound better?" She couldn't believe Jerome right now. "So, what am I supposed be, Mac's slave for the weekend?"

Jerome slumped down on the edge of the bed and put his head in his hands. "I don't know, Carman…" He murmured, more to himself then her. He peered up into her eyes. "If you refuse to participate, he'll kill me."

"What?" Just when she thought the news couldn't get any worse. "Mac can't do that-- he's blackmailin' you." She pressed him to call the police and file charges. Jerome shook his head in despair. "No, this is deeper than blackmail. My life is at stake here. It's a deal we agreed on, and if I don't follow through, he will make good on his word" he lamented. Jerome wouldn't only lose his life, they would lose their house. He was already late on the mortgage.

"Mac said if you comply with da arrangement, that at da end of da weekend he'll return my losses" he told her, leaving out the part about the watch.

Carman was boiling with anger. Losing all the month's pay, and then expecting her to be some sort of slave to Mac Shaun. She went over to the bed and collected a pillow and duvet and threw them at Jerome. She was so pissed she couldn't even look at his face. Later that night, while lying awake in bed, Carman considered her husband predicament. If she went through with the arrangement, knowing full well it would involve sex with another man, she wondered if their marriage could survive such a thing. Could Jerome handle knowing his wife of six years spent the weekend with another man, someone he would see on the regular? If she refused, Jerome would die. She knew that for sure. Jerome had not only put his life in danger, but their home and marriage too. That's what pissed Carman off the most, that Jerome would risk so much over a game of poker.

On second thought, thinking about Mac Shaun, Carman had to admit he was handsome, despite him being a killer and all. Tall and dark, with an athletic build. He was in his mid-thirties, intelligent, charismatic, with a pleasant sense of humor. They had crossed paths a couple times in the neighborhood. He was a very attractive man with deep dish waves that any woman would love to run her fingers through. Carman felt flattered he would make a deal to spend the weekend with her. She didn't know the man that well, however. What if he was some sort of sexual deviant? Carman got tired of thinking about it, so she rolled and went to sleep with a smile on the corner of her lips.

Chapter Two

* * * * *

Friday evening, just before seven o'clock, Carman arrived at Mac's apartment wearing a Prada wrap-around dress, that fit snugly around her midriff and matching red bottoms complimented the black velvet. Before knocking on the door, Carman nervously adjusted herself and waited. She knew once she entered the apartment, her marriage would never be the same again. Mac answered the door with an amicable smile. He checked her out, taking in the enticing sight of her nubile breasts held up by the wrap-around bodice.

"Hello, Carman, you look exceptional this evenin'. Please come in and let me take that for you" he said as he reached for her overnight bag, and closed the door behind her. Carman followed as Mac led the way through the front room, down the hall to the living room. The bedroom was spacious with a large bed, walk-in closet, and matching furniture. Mac placed her bag on the foot of the bed, then faced her. He was dressed smart in a black and gray Polo button up shirt and a pair of custom jeans. Mac extended a large hand from across the room. "Let me help you to da car so we can be on our way" he offered. Carman wondered where they could be going at this instant. He escorted her to the elevator. Carman was breathtaking, of mahogany complexion, 5'9" with 34-28-34 measurements. She was in her late twenties, beautiful, but still a bit naive. In the passenger seat, Carman noticed the strong fragrance of his expensive cologne.

"Where are we goin'?" she finally asked.

He glanced over while driving. "To a lounge for some drinks, conversation, and if you like, dancin'."

It wasn't quite what she had expected, but then again Carman had no idea what to expect from Mac Shaun. At the red light, he looked at Carmen's delicate profile. "I trust Jerome has explained da conditions of this liaison?"

She couldn't help but scoff in full disdain. She crossed her arms and stared straight ahead without answering.

"You may not believe this right now, but this weekend is more about you."

"What is that supposed to mean?" she asked.

"In order for that to happen you must be willin' to comply. Compliance is da most important thang. Acquiescence and everythang will be fine."

Carman threw Mac an indignant glance. She thought he might be threatening her. Suggesting if she didn't do whatever he wanted, he would kill Jerome. If she didn't, he would surely kill Jerome. They entered an upscale club on the East Side of Milwaukee, and into a privacy booth alongside the wall. He ordered them some libations. As he sipped his Martini, he gazed into Carman's eyes.

"What is your favorite sexual position?" he asked.

Carman almost choked on her sweet alcohol thinking he was beyond rude and inconsiderate. "Excuse me?"

Mac smiled as he admired the gold rims floating in her irises. "Your favorite position?" he repeated. "Or do you have more than just one?"

"I..." She wasn't sure how to reply.

"Come on, Carman" he pressured her, becoming impatient.

"We both know why you're here, and what da arrangement is goin' to lead to, so what's da point of bein' coy? I'll be honest with you. I've been attracted to you for a long time. From da first time we met. But you fuck wit Jerome's soft ass, and I consider him to be sort of a friend, so I never shot at you. But when this opportunity came, I knew I had to take full advantage of it. Because I might never get da chance again. I'm neither here to babysit nor seduce. Da choice is yours; and I'm not goin' to keep remindin' you why you're here. I won't ask you twice. Either you make da choice, or else" he made himself clear. Carman acknowledged him with a simple nod. "I don't have only one favorite position. I enjoy being hit from da back doggy style, allowin' my partner to control the depth and rhythm. I enjoy being spooned, feelin' a large hand run over my body while being hit from behind. And, of course, being on top, where I'm in control."

Mac took another sip of his drink and smiled. "I appreciate your honesty, Carman. Does size matter?"

She cocked her eyebrow and quipped. "Self-conscious, are we?"

"Nah, I can assure you I'm quite comfortable with my size" he answered.

Carman took a sip of her drink, surprised how she opened up so fast to flirting, and batting her long eyelashes. "Size is not the most important thing—I mean, it's good if the man is well-endowed—but not all that important" To her, it depended on how well he worked his... tool.

Mac gave her a "knowingly bullshit" smirk. "So, you'd be pleased with just three inches?"

Now Carman tossed her head back and laughed. "That would be uncomfortable."

Mac explored Carman with his gluttonous gaze She possessed beauty and elegance, with a slight touch of coquettish humor that made her all the more alluring. "So, you prefer larger?"

"Not too big. Somethin' that won't be too uncomfortable and leave me sore."

"What is your ideal size?" he contined.

She took a moment to ponder. "Somethin' above average size. Perhaps eight—eight and a half."

Mac nodded. "You like to suck dick?"

"I enjoy givin' as well as receivin'?" she admitted, feeling playful.

"Deep throat?" he asked.

Carman's mind began to race. "If it's not too big..." she conceded, feeling a distinctive heat descend to her loins, and her nipples hardened. Mac noticed her arousal. Her nipples poked through her dress. "Do you do anal?"

"I..." she blushed. "Haven't indulged in a long time."

"Did you enjoy it when you did?" He could see the desire rekindling in the depths of her eyes.

"I enjoyed it with my boyfriend before I met Jerome."

"He doesn't indulge that?"

"I suggested it once, but he refused. He thinks it's dirty."

Mac shook his head. "That is a shame. I believe a woman's desires, no matter how dissolute they may be, should be explored and fulfilled. That's what I want to do with you, Carman." The declaration took her by surprise. "I want to explore and breach da walls of your inhibitions. Bring you to da very edge of ecstasy and cast you into da depths of delirious rapture. I want to make you cum, watch you squirm in da throes of delectation, until your body isn't able to take any more."

No one had ever spoken to her like this. Carman found it very erotic. Like I said on da ride over here, this weekend is more about you rather than me. I'm sure you imagined that I simply want to fuck and discard you. I assure you, Carman, that's never been my intention. Have you ever been with a woman?"

"Excuse me?" she responded, clearly taken aback.

"Have you ever been with another women?" he asked her again, showing his deviant smile.

"Briefly, while in college. A roommate and I slept together once. Had a threesome with her boyfriend—it was his birthday gift."

"Just once?" he wondered.

Carman nodded. "Dumb nigga ended up cheatin' on Crystal when he had everthang at home. She dumped him. Not long after, I met Trent. He took my anal cherry. We only dated for like six months, then I met Jerome. Two years later, we got married."

Mac shifted his weight on the red vinyl cushion. "Tell me about your fantasies" he pried, taking a sip of his Martini and watching her. Carman spoke with a gracious dip of her slender wrist. "Oh, I don't know. Guess they're pretty basic, really. I'd like to have sex in a public place. Maybe try some light bondage—"

"Come on, Carman" he urged, cutting her off. "I ain't talkin' bout what all woman wanna have. Tell me about what you fantasize about while you're masturbatin' and makin' luv. Da image that sends you over da edge each time" he crooned. What she was about to reveal, Carman had never disclosed to anyone. "I fantasize about havin' a threesome… sometimes with another woman, most times with two men. Being taken by both back and forth… at the same time. But there is one fantasy that I've always had since I was a little girl…"

"Oh?" Mac inquired.

"It goes back to when I was in junior high. Some friends and I were goofin' off in class and I was sent to the principal's office. Havin' never been in trouble before, I was really frightened. I sat there nervously in the hall waitin' my turn to be called in. When I did, Principal Drew gave me a stern lecture and warnin'. Even when as far as sayin' that back in the old days he used to take naughty girls over his lap, lift their skirts, and deliver a thorough spankin'. Seated across from his desk, something about the image hangin' over his lap and being spanked excited me. I imagined Principal Drew liftin' my skirt, his large hand rising and comin' down on my behind, over and over. How each slap would make me squirm and cry. Then he would stand me up and bend me over his desk and take me from behind." Talking about this made her silk thong soaking wet. Mac listened with fingers intertwined in front of his lips. "You want to be spanked like a naughty schoolgirl?"

"Not just spanked" Carman corrected. "Spanked and fucked. Specifically bent over a desk" she stated. "At the time, I really didn't know anythang about sex, but the images were stuck in my mind and they turned into my fantasy."

"Have you ever been spanked?" he asked her. Carman shook her head. Mac smiled at Carman. "You're wet just talkin' about it all, aren't you?"

He put her on the spotlight. She crossed her thighs and glanced down to look at the prominent tips of her erect nipples. When she looked up again, she noticed Mac watching her.

"Yes" she answered, unable to deny the obvious. *Soaked was more like it*, she thought to herself.

Mac collected their glasses and slides from the booth. "While I go and replenish our drinks, why don't you go to da bathroom and remove your panties?" Carman did as Mac requested and removed her thong. Then she exited the ladies' room feeling self-conscious about the cool air caressing her. She felt as if everyone was looking at her, as if they knew she had no underwear. She returned to the booth and found Mac waiting with their drinks. His gaze traveled up her legs and over the front of her skirt. Carman set down and quickly crosses her thighs. Mac sat up straight and extended his hand over the table. "Give them to me."

Carman opened her black clutch purse and retrieved the thong, and dropped it in Mac's open hand.

He didn't even look at it, but just merely stored it in his pocket. "Describe your pussy for me."

"Huh?" she asked, not quite sure what he meant by that.

"Do you leave it naturally hairy, trimmed, shaved or waxed?"

"Oh..." she replied. "Neatly trimmed on top and waxed below."

"Show me" he demanded.

"Here? Right now?" she asked, flustered.

"Yeah, stand up and show me... now" he commanded this time.

"In a public nightclub?" she asked, reticent

"Either that, or leave" he replied, his tone too dark for comfort.

Carman knew he was testing her. She uncrossed her legs and slid out of the vinyl seat. She took the hem of her skirt, and slowly, very slowly, pulled it up. She was praying no one would notice.

"Higher, please" he pressed on.

Carman was embarrassed, but lifted the dress up to her navel. Her thighs were parted slightly, showing off the distinctive gap. Ensconced between the gap were adipose lips, soft and smooth to the touch.

"That's very nice. I appreciate a woman who can take care of her pussy. And yours is pretty. You may sit down now" he said

She quickly smoothed down her dress and sat back in the booth. No one was watching. Her exposure had gone unnoticed. In a naughty sort of a way, she found it exciting.

"Would you like to dance, Carman?"

She took a drink. "Sure" she replied.

After a couple of songs, they returned to their booth. Carman headed again to the ladies' room. Without panties, her juices threatened to run down her thighs. When she returned to the booth, she finished off her drink. Mac drained his drink too. "Shall we go?"

During the drive back to his apartment, Carman stared silently out the passenger window. Deep down, she dreaded this moment. She didn't know what to expect, but she knew it involved sex. All she could do was pray the adultery wouldn't ruin her marriage.

Chapter Three

* * * * *

Once inside the apartment, Mac led Carman to the bedroom. Carman stood anxiously at the foot of the bed. She hadn't felt the urge to bite her fingernails since she was a teen; but right now it took every fiber of her being not to put her fingertips in her mouth. Mac exited the closet in just his Gucci boxers. "Take off your dress" he ordered her.

Carman fingers trembled apprehensively as she untied the sash that secured the dress to her midriff. She slowly unwrapped it from her slim waist. She was naked, she wasn't even wearing a bra. The only man that had seen her nude over the past eight years had been Jerome. It was his fault that she was here now. She had to pay his gambling debt with her body. Mac watched as Carman pulled her slender arms from the short sleeves and exposed her full back. He ran his gaze up along the back of her toned calves, her thick thighs, and the fullness of her ample buttocks. Its rotunda shape was accentuated by the curved hips and slim waist. "Turn around, Carman" he said.

She gulped audibly and turned around slowly. Her breasts heaved. Deep down, she wished she had the fortitude to flee, and say the hell with Mac Shaun... but there was too much at stake. Starting from the painted tips of her toenails, Mac slowly traced his gaze over the surface of Carman's feet, shins, and knees. Her thighs were pressed together. Her Aphrodite figure accentuated the black triangle of hairs, toned abdomen, slender arms, upturned dark areolas and taut nipples. Her jet-black hair hung behind her shoulders. She waited; apprehensive and timid.

"Carman" he called to her. She looked up and captured the gaze of his brown eyes that locked with hers. "You're incredibly gorgeous" he complimented. She was a dark-haired creation of exquisite beauty. Mac stepped closer and touched the soft curve of Carman's shoulder. She flinched. "You have nothin' to fear, Carman" he eased her. What he planned on doing would leave her panting in the aftermath of delirious pleasure. "Have a seat, please" he directed her to the edge of the bed. Carman sat down. Mac went over to retrieve a chair and took a seat in front of her.

"Lean back and relax" he ordered her. He placed his hands atop her knees and eased her thick thighs apart. He bowed over and planted an affectionate kiss along the top of her left leg. He placed her calf over his shoulder that made her lean back. He trailed soft kisses along the smooth, sensitive skin of her inner thigh. He lazed his way to the outer part of her pussy, then worshiped the other inner thigh. Carman tried hard not to squirm. She bit her lip to keep from uttering moans. Her hips squirmed as his warm breath caressed the bare surface of her outer labia. It was wrong to enjoy what was happening. Shouldn't she feel guilty for it? She asked herself. Her body was betraying her resolve, beginning to respond in close proximity of Mac's mouth next to her pussy.

It had been a long time since Jerome went down on her. He always wanted his dick sucked, but was short on returning the favor. The way she saw it, a fair exchange wasn't no robbery. Mac's soft kisses ascended the sensitive skin of her right inner thigh, causing the volume of her hillocks to swell with heated desire. Mac lowered his face between her parted thighs and planted a soft kiss over the adipose tissues, which elicited a loud moan from Carman. He extended the tip of his wet tongue and ran it up and down both pussy lips. He ran his tongue right up the slit, digging under, flicking across her salient clitoris. Carman gasped as an electrical jolt of pleasure shot through her. Desire permeated into the depths of her trembling vagina, causing her vulva to gasp open. He grasped the back of her knees and pulled her thighs wide apart.

Mac used his thumbs to spread the wrinkles of her thick pussy lips and exposing the cotton pink hole. Holding the lips wide open, he pursed his lips to blow a slow stream of air over the glistening surface. The puckered brim of her pussy hole contracted, and she moaned and squirmed. Tear drops of sweet juices leaked. The aphrodisiacal scent of her pussy filled Mac's nose. With his tongue, he captured the descending rivulet of the dripping honey. He savored the silky texture of her sweet syrup in his mouth. With her knees pushed back toward her shoulders, Carman leaned back on her elbows and peered down over her heaving bosom. She watched Mac leisurely explore her pussy with the tip of his tongue. The exquisite sensation caused her toes to curl. Palms down by her sides, Carman grasped two handfuls of the Egyptian cotton bed sheets as Mac pushed his tongue inside her clinching vulva. She tilted her head back and moaned even louder.

Her hillocks clamped tightly around the squishy organ invading her. His tongue moved inside her. Carman began to pump her hips while moaning uncontrollably, wrenching in pure pleasure. Tongue fucking her juicy pussy, Mac used the thumb of his left hand to stimulate her salient clitoris. He pinched the raised flesh and rubbed it back and forth. Stimulating the nerves in her clitoris, he replaced his fingers with his tongue. Taking the pink pearl in his mouth and sticking his middle finger in her pussy, he made Carman moan. Her pussy clamped tightly around his digits as she gripped the sheets. "Right there..." she panted; getting her pussy eaten was a duty her husband had neglected far too long. He slid two fingers and found her G-spot while flicking his tongue over her tented hood. It drove her crazy with pleasure. She bridged her pelvis, trying to reach her blissful release. "Oh God... Oh God!" she cried out. Her body spasmed, suspending a crest wave of orgasms. She was almost out of breath, but she bucked and thrashed on the verge of passing out. She couldn't remember the last time she climaxed so hard, if ever. Once the muscular contractions eased between Mac fingers, he pulled them out and lowered his mouth to lap up the flow of her juices. Once he was done, he undressed. Carman leaned up on her elbows to watch Mac. She admired his muscular physique. Dark hair ran across his wide chest and down to the pit of his navel. She held her breath as he bent over and dropped his boxers. At the club, Mac had quipped about being well-endowed. Now, she figured it had to be at least eight inches dangled before her. Didn't all men boast about having this? It was clear Mac was extremely modest. Mac was hung like a porn star and larger than Jerome. She could only imagine him hard. Mac smiled at Carman's shocked expression and stepped towards her. "Does it please you, Carman?"

She swung her legs over the edge of the bed and nodded... dumbfounded. She couldn't take her eyes from his midsection. "It's incredible..." she murmured wrapping her hand around the meat and stroking it. A surge of blood rushed into the tubular chambers and he hardened in her hand. He surged to eleven inches. She couldn't believe the monster before her. Carman encircled the trunk with her forefinger and thumb, staring at it in awe at the towering prominence. If she was an artist, she would draw the perfect embodiment of masculinity. Mac's dick was a model in her eyes. The circumference was so wide, she couldn't fit her hand completely around it.

She tucked her hair behind her ear and stuck out her tongue, catching the pre-cum that formed at the tip. She relished his dick, running her tongue up and down the surface and the bulging veins. Savoring it like a popsicle, she coated it with her saliva, running her tongue around the dark helmet and opened her mouth wide. When Carman first arrived at Mac's apartment, she knew what would be expected. She had asked herself if she was made to suck him off. She would gag a lot and acted as if she didn't know what she was doing. And if he laid her down, she would just lay there till he got it over with. But now, here she was pleasuring him, with no resistance and a huge dick in her mouth, the tip ensconced at the entrance of her throat. The top of his engorged head against the roof of her mouth. Sucking him to the base, she hollowed her cheeks and receded along the shaft. She held the glans' ridge just inside her lips and swirled her slippery wet tongue around its velvet skin. She emitted soft moans in delight. Tingling vibrations coursed through his body. The salty tang of pre-cum tantalized her taste buds. The flavors elicited a moan from her.

While holding Mac's dick in her mouth, she looked up at him through her hazel eyes. She sucked the meat slowly in and out of her wet mouth. Her cheeks indented as she sucked long and hard. Only breaking the seal of vacuity to slurp him. Carman breathed in and out as her head pistoned slowly. She sucked him deep, her nose touching his pubic hair. She savored every creamy drop, concentrated in making him cum. Then, she needed him in her hungry pussy. Unable to wait any longer, Carman popped his dick from her hungry mouth. His freed erection sprung up and hit his lower abdomen. It sounded like a wet rag against a wall. Smiling mischievously, she turned on her hips to proposition herself on the bed. With one heel on the foot of the bed and the other over his shoulder, she reached down and guided his manhood toward her soaked pussy. As she reclined back, Carman was watching Mac pushing forward. The glans extended a pliant vulva and entered her moist chambers. Carman tilted her head back and closed her eyes in exquisite pleasure. She released moan. His thick dick slid into her. As he pushed in, he adjusted her leg on his shoulder. This opened Carman wider. His burrowed meat touched regions that Jerome's had never reached. Mac watched the pure rapture on her pretty face. Her eyes rolled in throes as he stretched her. He began to rock his hips, pumping the length of his dick in and out of her. He wanted to fuck her ever since he saw her. Mac savored each stroke, fucking her luscious pussy slow and easy. Carman began to lift her hips too match each of his strokes. His ball sack smacked her anus. She peered down watching his shiny shaft entering her, filling her pussy over and over and stimulating the plush walls of her vulva. Mac released her shin and extracted himself from her. To lay beside her to spoon. He held her thigh as he directed his head to her wet hole. Then pushed inside her, making her moan. He pushed her hair back from her elegant neck and gave her sensitive skin amorous love bites. He was running his large hand over her soft breasts, squeezing and kneading the fullness while pumping in and out of her tight pussy. Carman placed her foot behind Mac's legs and groaned in sensual pleasure. Sighs of pleasure emitted as he rubbed his hand up and down her body. She pushed back to meet his deep penetration, liking it. She tilted her head back to give him an affectionate kiss. His dick pushed deeply inside her. She gasped as Mac's hand cupped her labia and began to rub her engorged clitoris.

"Oooooh..." she crooned as his thumb manipulated the pink bud. That was all it took to make her cum. She went over the edge gasping, moaning, and shuddering in waves that rippled through her. Mac was buried deep, allowing Carman to enjoy her climax in full. He rubbed her clit, pinched her erect nipples and bit her neck softly. Once her violent shaking of delectation subsided, Mac rolled Carman onto her stomach. Never breaking the union of his dick from her, he was then guiding her onto her hands and knees. He enveloped her slim waist in his large hands and began stroking her lubed pussy from behind. Strands of Carman's jet-black hair hung down her shoulders. She pushed back meeting his strokes. Taking every inch of his driving tool, it felt even more wonderful in the current position. His length nudged her cervix over and over. She groaned and moaned with every expansion of her vulva. Forcefully, she went down on her forearms as he pounded her from behind, making her heart-shaped ass round out and jiggle with each pump. Mac watched as his lance slid in and out of her hot pussy. The thin layer of brown skin protracted along the slick surface of his shaft. Every time he retracted, he did so only the tip was left inside. Then he shoved to the halt. Giving her long strokes in opulence over and over.

"Mmmm, yesss...!" Carman moaned looking over her shoulder as Mac plowed her. She panted in sheer admiration from the sensation. Reaching underneath, she cupped herself and diddled her clit. "Fuck me, fuck me!" she screamed, lost in the throes of sexual pleasure. Mac gripped her hips tightly as he began to fuck her faster. Thrusting deep and hard, just as she begged. Their flesh met violently, resounding smacks. His jostling balls slapped her puffy lips of her labium. He panted while he was piledriving into her. Carman cried out as she climaxed a second time. Mac rammed deep into her shuddering pussy. He groaned as a surge erupted from the eyelet. Pumping her with long streams of jism, semen, and coital fluid mixed together in a slurry. It breached the seal of her expanded vulva and runs down her inner thighs. Mac pulled out leaving her vacated hole yawning open. They collapsed, glistening in a sheen of sweat, and chests heaving.

Mac wasn't done with her yet. He pushed her head into his lap. Forcing her to suck his pussy cum coated dick back to life. Then he mounted her, savoring each stroke. They rolled over, letting her take control. Her hips rocked back and forth. Mac squeezed her breasts as she frantically rubbed her clit. Once Carman came down from her orgasmic high, Mac pinned her to the bed and fucked her hard, filling her with molten jism. The cum ran out of her, dripping down the crack of her spread ass hole.

Chapter Four

* * * * *

Carman awoke the following morning and blinked her long eyelashes in a temporary confusion of the strange room, then smiled in remembrance. Last night seemed like a wicked dream. She hadn't gotten laid like that in... come to think of it, she never had been thoroughly fucked like that before. Usually after her husband's bust, he was spent for the night. Not Mac, though. He was a sex machine. They did all her favorite positions in a single night, and she came each time. It was a record five times in one night. She looked over at Mac, watching him sleep. Her thoughts drifted home. She began to wonder what Jerome was doing right now. Was he sleeping? Or was he lying awake wondering about her first night with another man? He could be regretting what he'd done. At first, Carman was incensed at her husband when she found out that his dumb ass wagered her and lost his monthly salary at a poker game. It was that very anger that led her to spend the weekend with Mac Shaun. Though Jerome's life was in jeopardy, she also did it to teach Jerome a lesson.

Last night while having drinks at the nightclub with Mac, Carman discovered it was Mac who set up Jerome. He'd manipulated the opportunity to be with her. She found it kind of flattering that someone would scheme like that to have her. After all, Mac turned out to be like no one she'd ever known. Very open, direct, and honest. Not to mention charming, funny, and incredibly charismatic. At first she was overwhelmed by the situation, seeing it as a dilemma. Now she was glad. Mac stirred in his sleep and opened his light brown eyes. Finding Carman West staring at him amorously. He yawned and stretched then extended his hand to Carman, which she took obediently. He led her into the bathroom.

They showered together, taking turns washing each other down with a soapy towel. Mac admired Carman's smooth brown skin glistening in the running water. Rivulets of suds cascaded all over her body. He squeezed her 34 C-cups. Her hard nipples stood taut under the steaming shower head. Pushing her up against the tile wall, Mac pushed into her. Carman moaned loudly as he entered her. Their hums echoed over the running water, bouncing off the bathroom walls. Carman's fingernails scraped the aqua blue tiles and her back squeaked along the surface as he fucked her against the wall. He was pushing all eleven inches in her as he slid into her tender pussy. She was a little sore from the previous night but welcomed the aching discomfort.

"Ahh yeah, fuck me, daddy!" she pleaded. He filled her completely. He fucked her and had her cumming in rivers. She trembled up against the tiles, triggering his orgasm. He blasted off inside her, causing her to cum again as her pussy was pumped full of jism.

* * * * *

Wearing only a thong and Mac's buttoned up shirt, Carman stood over the stove preparing breakfast. Mac sat at the table checking his messages on his cellphone.

"I have to visit a friend later in the mornin'" he announced as Carman served him an omelet. "When I return, be ready to go. We'll dine out. While I'm gone, I expect you to clean da place, drop off and pick up my dry cleaners. Da slip is on da dresser in da closet" he told her. Normally, she would have told a man to go fuck himself. But after the pleasure he provided her last night, she obediently agreed. "Alright, daddy." Plus, she knew he wouldn't take no for an answer.

"You'll find fresh bed linen in da hall closet, along with da feather duster and vacuum. Da cleanin' products are under da kitchen sink."

"Alright."

"I'll leave money for da dry cleanin' and Uber fare. I'll be back in da afternoon."

After Mac left, Carman did the dishes, cleaned the kitchen and the rest of the penthouse apartment. She noticed Mac had fine taste in art. Black history and literature books filled the shelves. After cleaning, Carman booked an Uber, and dropped off Mac's weekly dry cleaning. There was an empty rack in the walk-in closet, as if a section of clothes had been removed; so she placed his clothes there. Back in the living room, she tuned in to Atlanta Housewives and curled up on the couch.

Chapter Five

* * * * *

Carman stirred to the sound of a woman's laughter as Mac walked in. She sat up and yawned, stretching her arms above her head. She hadn't realized she drifted off. Mac led the woman through the vestibule. The woman was attractively dressed in a pair of Michael Kors heels and red Michael Kors dress. She was also very exquisite in an elegant way. With a voluminous mane of reddish brown hair and hazel eyes. She had the color of honey complexion. A natural tan from being in the sun. Mac led the beautiful woman over to her.

"Carman, this is my friend, Kim" he said. The ladies' eyes roved over each other.

"Carman, why don't u go freshen up?" Mac ordered, noticing she had been asleep. "Then join me and Kim."

When Carman returned from the bathroom, she peeked into the bedroom from the hall. Kim was down on her knees sucking Mac's dick. Her skirt was hiked up around her waist, while she finger fucked her twat. Mac heard Carman in the hallway as she gasped in shock. While he fucked Kim's face, he called Carman to join. "You wanted to have a threesome with another woman. So does Kim, so come in here and join us."

At first, Carman felt a twinge of jealousy discovering another woman adoring the dick that was supposed to be hers for the weekend. But watching Kim pop Mac's dick from her mouth, all glistening from her saliva, and offering a welcoming smile, somehow pushed the jealousy away. Carman walked in and knelt next to Kim. Maybe this was a dream. She was still asleep on the couch and wasn't here at all. That's what she wanted to blame her actions on; but she knew this was reality. Kim aimed Mac's erection at Carman's lips, and she sucked it in. All the way to the base. The women took turns sucking him back and forth. Kissing each other amorously in between turns. Kim ran her thumb up the underside of his meat and milked a clear drop of pre-cum from the eyelet. Then dabbed the syrupy fluid with the pad of her index finger. Bringing the finger to Carman lips, she sucked it off with an audible moan. The girls kissed as they removed each other's clothes.

They'd just met barely twenty minutes ago, then they were sucking dick together and kissing. Carman could hardly believe it. How long had it been since the last time she was with another woman? It had been her roommate in college, Crystal Jennings. What had begun as curious touching and kissing, eventually led to a threesome with her boyfriend, Big Mike. That was over eight years ago. Carman asked Jerome if he would ever want to be with another woman, but he said no. He told her she was all the woman he ever needed. Carman thought all guys had fantasies of being with two women, but Jerome was too old-fashioned for that. So, she never asked again. Carman unzipped the back of Kim's dress.

She was nude. Kim stood beautifully before her. Their matching measurements of 34-28-34 were astounding, with the exception of one different asset... Kim was a 34D. Carman smiled at Kim's upturned crown of her pink areolas and hard nipples. She looked down at reddish-brown triangle between Kim's legs. She led Kim to the bed, then joined her. She was then kissing her while tracing her thumb down Kim's body and kneading her breasts., Kim moaned feeding her nipple into Carnan's mouth. Carman sucked adoringly, swirling her tongue around the taut halo. Kim moaned in pure bliss. She loved having her tits licked and sucked. Foreplay was a major part of sex. Kim slid her hand down Carman's back, around her derrière, then to her mound. Carman groaned as Kim's hand touched her pussy. She pushed two fingers into Carman. Carman moaned in appreciation for the ministration Kim offered between her thighs.   She finger-fucked her, using her thumb to simultaneously diddle her clitoris. Kim worked her fingers in and out of Carman's slick pussy. Her fingers gliding through the smooth velvet lips. She collected a rich slather of juices, pulling her fingers from Carman, and pushed her fingers into Carman's mouth. Carman sucked them hungrily with her lips pursed, and eyes closed as she swirled her tongue around the digits. When Carman pulled herself away from Kim's fingers, she stuck her tongue in Kim's mouth, sharing the sweet flavors of her pussy juices. She trailed her way down Kim's body, leaving a slick trail of saliva. It had been too damn long since she had eaten pussy. She planted an amorous kiss on her slit. Then trailed her tongue up the plump labia and down the left side. Stiffening her tongue, she pushed into Kim's cotton candy pink slit. The first taste was sweet, decadent.

Kim reached down and spread her pussy lips open, giving Carman more access to her.

Carman licked her, teasing the nub, and they both shifted around to form a 69. While doing so, Mac began to undress as they ate each other. He watched closely, standing at the edge of bed stroking his erection, watching Kim's tongue dart in and out of Carman's pussy. The curtains of Carman's jet-black hair spilled over the edge of the mattress. While shoving her tongue in Kim's love hole, the girls felt the weight of Mac's knee down on the mattress. He was finally getting involved. Carman's heart fluttered. Her dream was finally coming true. Carman stopped eating Kim's pussy long enough to look over to see Mac's dick near her. She took hold of Mac's dick and aligned it with Kim's opening. Mac eased his way into Kim. Kim responded to the penetration by lifting her from the succulent snatch and moaned. The length and width of Mac's dick expanded her vaginal tract.

Carman held the side of Kim's slim waist, watching Mac thick vein dick pistoning in and out of her. Every time he pulled out, his piece glistened with a glossy film of pussy juice. The oily texture provided a smooth coating for his shaft. He drew back to the tip, then pushed all the way in. Kim scoffed in pleasure. While he fucked her, Carman licked Kim's dangling clitoral hood, making her moan out loud. With one knee on the bed, he pressed down on Kim's firm ass, pumping the length of his dick in and out of her wet tunnel. Her plush walls were smooth as velvet. Just below his ball sack Carman lapped up the copious juices that formed around on his dick and Kim's pussy. Mac removed his dick then pushed it into Carman's succulent mouth. Her mouth wrapped around his dick coated in Kim's juice. She sucked and matched his strides as he began to fuck her face, grabbing the back of her head as he shoved it down her throat. Kim crawled up to the headboard and reclined. Mac pulled out of Carman's mouth and forced her to her knees. She crawled over to Kim, who still had her heels on. The heels slanted on the bed with her thighs spread wide. Her nipples pointed upward. Kim reached down and spread her pussy lips. "Eat my pussy, bitch" she demanded.

Carman had never let another person call her a bitch and get away with it. She was from the hood; and that word called for an ass whooping. But for some reason, she was turned on. The illusion of being dominated really did it for her. Mac rubbed his dick up and down her slit while she went down on Kim. At the same time, Mac slid into Carman from behind. She crossed her knees, compressing the thick dick in her vulva. With one hand placed on the plump of Carman's ass, he could see the length piston in and out of her hot pussy. Carman moaned in pleasure, never letting up on eating Kim's pussy. Mac picked up the pace and fucked her faster.

Carman began to pant, moaning out loudly. "Oh, oooooohhhh!" she screamed brought to a wonderful orgasm while arching her ass higher. Pulling out of her, Mac presented his dick to Kim. Kim took his creamed dick in her mouth and sucked for dear life. She sucked him delicately, until he pulled away out of fear of busting too soon. His dick sprang up against his lower abdomen. When he recuperated, he aimed at her pussy hole. She reached down and spread her lips with two fingers.

"Ooooooooooh" she cooed salaciously as the thick length of Mac's meat invaded her. Kim began to rub her clit, watching him fuck her. It added to the excitement that she could witness his sausage slide in and out of her horned-up pussy. In the process, Carman offered her breast to her mouth; and Mac pushed his finger in Carman from behind. The scene of them engaging in a trio was so erotic. He worked his finger in her from behind. She closed her eyes and moaned in exquisite pleasure, as he pushed his middle finger in her ass. Then he was fingering her in her pussy and ass in sync. Kim took the opportunity to diddle her clitoris faster.

"Mmmm" Carman moaned in pure pleasure. If anything on earth was close to heaven, it was the feeling she was experiencing now. Her nipple was being sucked, her clit stimulated, and her pussy and ass fingered at the same time. "Oh, oh God…" It was an incredible sensation between the membrane dividing the rectum. Feeling Kim's knuckle on her knob, Mac fingered her ass and pussy in a contrapuntal motion. "Oh yes, yes..." she chanted. "You're makin' me cum…" she breathed going over the edge. It was like water overflowing from the cup. A heavy orgasm ripped through her. "Oh, ooh God... Yeeessss!" she exploded, shuddering.

With his fingers still buried in Carman's ass and pussy, he began to fuck Kim faster and harder, causing her breasts to jiggle like Jell-O. She could feel her own pressure rising. Still diddling Carman's clit, she came hard. Bucking, moaning and wrenching on the bed, while Mac pounded her contracting pussy. Her clenching pussy stimulated Mac's dick head, causing his jostling testicles to tense and catapult torrential streams of seminal fluid. He quickly pulled out, grabbed his pulsating dick, and jacked it off over Kim. The first shoot landed on Kim's heaving breast. The subsequent ejaculations spit forward and landed across her stomach.

Like a thirsty bitch, Carman licked off the opalescent tendrils and glob of cum off Kim's tits and stomach. The threesome was a hundred times better than the one she had eight years ago with Crystal and Big Mike. She knew for sure she wouldn't wait so long next time to fulfill her urge for pussy. Whether Jerome liked it or not, she would do as she pleased.

Chapter Six

* * * * *

After supper, while Carman cleared the table, Mac went and built a cozy fire and invited Carman over. They sat down and sipped some cognac. The fire illuminated the surface of their complexions like embers on a coal fire. Carman sat with her legs under her, enjoying the warmth of the crackling fire and the effect from the cognac.

"What?" she asked, a little self-conscious of Mac's steady gaze. Why was he staring at her like that?

"I'm just admirin' da elegance of fine beauty" he said. The compliment made Carman blush. She diverted her gaze like a demure schoolgirl. Mac smiled at her bashful reaction and reached over lifting Carman's chin. "I invited a friend over this evenin' to fulfill your fantasy with bein' with two men" he said looking straight into her eyes. A surprised expression filled her. "Why?"

"You don't want-"

"No, I want to, but why are you doing these things for me?" she asked.

Mac smiled. "When I first saw you two years ago on da block, I was immediately enthralled by your elegance and beauty. Most men that see a gorgeous woman think of how they want to fuck her. I on da other hand, when we first met, thought about how I would like to make your fantasies come true. I waited two years for this opportunity. I know you were angry under da conditions that brought you here. You probably only came out of spite. After convincin' yourself that it will be somethin' you'll just get it over with and done" he addressed her.

Carman averted her gaze downward. He was already reading her like an open book. He knew her too well.

"I knew if this weekend was dedicated to your pleasure, rather than an obligation to simply pay your husband's debt, you would be more comfortable and relaxed. I believe if you please a woman, she will be content, and will want to please you. I didn't want you to be on your guard. I don't want you to feel this is something you must get done and over with. I want to provide an opportunity for you to fulfill whatever desires you have. Because bein' with you is a fulfillment to me" he concluded.

Now Carman perfectly understood. Being with Mac was like no other man she had ever known. The depth of his understanding and consideration was very touching, giving a whole new light under which, she could admire him. He was a killer, but she felt she could fall in love with him. Mac checked the time on his cellphone and swallowed the remainder of his drink. "Tre should be here soon. I suggest you go use da bathroom. There is an enema bag under da sink" he told her.

Before Mac got up, Carman leaned over and gave him a kiss. It had been a long time since she had anal sex, but this was going to be even more exciting because she was fulfilling a long-time fantasy of being with two men.

* * * * *

Entering the living room, Carman found Mac on da couch next to a man with a well-groomed beard and perfect braids, he was dressed down in a Gucci suit. When they noticed her, they rose to greet her. "Carman" Mac introduced him to her. "This is my friend, Tre" he said. The man was tall and handsome, sort of resembling Nipsey Hussle—may he rest in peace. Carman smiled shyly at the vivid attention of his dark brown eyes. In her fantasy of being with two men, she had never put a face on any of them. But after tonight, her fantasy would be fulfilled.

"Hello, Tre" she said as she extended her slender hand. He took it, enveloping her small hand in his large palm. When he touched her, she began to imagine his hands roaming all over her body. Mac noticed the rise of her nipples.

Without a second thought, she undressed. She knew what she was here for, so there was no need for procrastination. The men watched her undress with sultry eyes. With no suggestion, they headed to the bedroom. Giddy with excitement, Carman had to control herself from running ahead of them to the bedroom. Her heart pumped anxiously, threatening to explode through her breast plate. Once in the room, Tre undressed. Carman smiled and her eyes widened at Tre's mesomorph body. He had washboard abs, a powerful chest, and broad shoulders. The big surprise came when he dropped his pants. He was even bigger than Mac. Her eyes bulged at the sight and wondered if she would fit him at all.

Carman sat on the edge of the bed and Tre stepped forward. She took his hose in the web of her palm and closed her slender fingers around the large schlong and began to pump the mighty python. Adding both hands to the fun, she jagged him slowly. Watching the head bulge with each pump, his penis began to enlarge. She took the head in her mouth and began to suck. She swirled her tongue around his head and the large balls. The girth of his large member expanded in her mouth completely stretching it. He was so thick, her finger wouldn't wrap around the girth, but that didn't stop her from sucking him in and out of her greedy mouth.

Mac got next to Tre. They stood shoulder to shoulder as he presented her with his hard dick. She took it in her fist and popped Tre's dick from her mouth to give Mac some attention. She sucked Mac and continued to stroke Tre's dick. Mac retracted his dick from her mouth, and they both gently eased her back on the bed. Their muscular hands were exploring her body, caressing and massaging her. Someone's lips encircled her nipple. When she looked down, she could see it was Mac's lips, and she moaned deep. Mac started to play with her clit. Carman spread her legs wide, while Tre planted kisses down her belly. Mac massaged and sucked on Carman's tits. Tre descended between her parted thighs. Carman reached down and spread herself wider while Tre traced along her outer folds. Carman squirmed and groaned, arching her back to push more of Tre's tongue into her wet hole. Tre really knew what he was doing.

Tre moved his hand and held her silky brown petals open with his thumb and forefinger. His long tongue delved up the crease of her sweet honey pot, lapping up the nectar. He captured her clitoris between his lips and stuck his middle finger inside her.

"Ooh, oh God!" Carman screamed as she climaxed, clenching her pussy muscles around his middle finger as she came. His finger pumped in and out of her, and he sucked at her clit. She moaned like she was being ravaged and torn apart.

Before she could calm down, Tre crawled between her parted legs, and started slowly inserting his twelve-inch member inside her. Tre began to pump his foot long in and out of her, while Mac shoved his dick in her mouth. As Tre penetrated her, she moaned around Mac's dick. She sucked hard as Mac fed her his dick in and out of her mouth. Tre plowed her while she kept orgasming. Her pussy felt overly stuffed by his size. She wrapped her legs behind his back, and began to rock her hips. He held her slender shins in his large hands stroking his monster dick in and out of her luscious pussy.

Both men removed their tools, leaving Carman gaping open, as they helped her on her hands and knees. There, they refilled her. Mac back in her mouth and Tre in her pussy. On her hands and knees, they seesawed her, taking one big dick after another. Tre had his hand around her waist, Mac had the back of her head. Soon, the men switched positions. Tre pulled out of her and she quickly spun around; so she could have her gaping hole refilled. She took Tre's dick in her mouth, while sticking her ass up like a bitch in heat. Mac slid into her hungry pussy. She sucked Tre's dick slathered in her own juices. She savored her flavors on him.

Mac quickly noticed how loose her pussy was from being stretched by Tre's thicker dick. He wasn't intimidated in any way. He was quite secure with his manhood. Mac sawed his shaft in and out of her creamy orifice. He watched as he drew in and out of her. She rotated her hips, pushing back to match his strokes. Again, they switched positions. Carman straddled Tre and began pumping her hips. She rode Tre fast and hard like a professional equestrian. Mac stood back and watched as Carman impaled herself on his friend. She gyrated her hips seductively on Tre's groin. Tre reached up and cup her breasts and squeezed. Carman moaned with her head thrown back in exquisite pleasure. Grinding her hips up and down Tre's pole, Mac left the room unnoticed. When he returned, he came with jar of vaseline. Carman was bucking Tre at full speed. Panting and moaning. Suddenly, her body tensed, arching her narrow back. She came, wailing in pleasure.

She cried out to the Lord while Tre kept pumping her tense body up and down his dick. When she calmed down, she collapsed forward on his chest. panting and gasping like runner, and they kissed very passionately. Mac crawled behind her upturned alabaster ass. Her pussy was bulging around the girth of Tre's dick. Mac spread her ass cheeks open. Coaxing a depleted moan from Carman, he noticed her anus peeking out. He applied a nice amount of Vaseline to her wrinkled rosette. Then slathered a glib on his dick. He entered her while sphincter gave resistance to being breached.

Carman raised her head from Tre's shoulder and moaned. It felt like stinging needles laced through her ass hole. "Owwwww!" she uttered her pain. But she didn't tell him to stop. The pain was so good. The mixture of pain and intimate pleasure made her toes curl. "Oh baby, I can feel both of you touching inside me" she panted.

Both dicks were only separated by the thin membrane of her stretched skin. Both her holes were stretched like the figure eight. Mac began sliding gently in and out of her greased ass hole. When Carman pushed up to accommodate Mac, she rose to the tip of Tre's massive dick. They began to move in a contrapuntal motion. One after the other, they rammed her in concert. They moved in a rhythm, patiently stabbing her with their passion. Carman pressed down on Tre's shoulder. Her breast pressed firmly, enjoying the sensation of both men.

"I—I'm going to cuuumm..." her body trembled. "I'm cumming! Yessssss, I'm cumming!"

The orgasm rippled through her rectum and vagina. Heightening the apex of her incredible orgasm, wave after wave flowed throughout her. Sandwiched between both men, she pumped herself frantically on their dicks. When her desire abated, she sighed heavily. Mac adjusted her from behind, rising her up on her knees, taking firm possession of her hips and began to plow into her tight ass. Tre squeezed her breasts and pinched her nipple. She moaned. She raised up and down on Tre's meat while Mac pushed deep into her ass. She reached down to diddle her swollen clit. The men increased the tempo, making her pant and gasp. As they ravished her, she collapsed on Tre's chest and climaxed again. Panting and moaning in the throes of orgasmic elation.

With one arm wrapped around Carman's waist, Mac shoved to the halt and began to shudder. Cumming deep in

Carman's ass, he released so much jism released it started seeping out of her hole. Tre hardened and shot his load into Carman's-soaked pussy. Carman cried out from the molten cum splattering against her cervix. The sensation drove her to another violent orgasm that left her convulsing.

* * * * *

The trio detached, and Carman went to the bathroom to freshen up. Returning, she sucked and stroked them both hard. The guys took turns fucking Carman. They had Carman position herself on her hands and knees. Her feet hung over the bed. The guys played a game of twenty strokes, trying to see who could make her cum the fastest. Mac pumped in her fast and hard twenty times. Just as he pulled out, Tre quickly replaced him to take his turn. This went on, until Mac won. She came. "Oooh, yeessssss!" she howled, clawing at the bed sheets.

After making her cum, they double penetrated her again. This time with Mac on the bottom. Tre fucked her tight ass hole. They fucked her without mercy until she passed out. Later that night, while laying sandwiched between the two masculine bodies, Carman smiled to herself and rolled over to snuggle with Mac. It was incredible. Far better then she had imagined. It was the type of sex she wanted with Jerome. She wanted to explore hidden desires, but he wasn't open to such possibilities. This made her realize what she was missing in her marriage, and what must change.

Chapter Seven

* * * * *

S unday afternoon, Carman packed her overnight bag. She recalled how she had stuffed her clothes in angry resentment towards Jerome. But now she was repacking it with regret and disappointment that the weekend had come to an end. Mac Shaun had turned out to be the most incredible man she'd ever known. Despite the fact he was a killer, he was the best lover she ever had. She never imagined how much she would regret leaving him. If Mac asked her to leave Jerome and stay, it would be too great of a temptation to refuse.

"Carman!" Mac called from the den.

"Yes!" she answered respectfully as she followed his voice down the hall. Mac sat behind a large mahogany desk. Ask me to stay and I will, she thought as she entered his study.

"Bring me a glass of Remy" he ordered her.

"Sure" she complied, going out to the mini bar and fixed him a drink.

"What's this?" he asked when she returned, holding the glass up.

"Brandy" she responded.

Mac held the glass out to her to take back. "I didn't ask for brandy, I asked for Remy" he demanded.

Carman chuckled nervously and stopped as she was confronted by Mac's serious glare.

"There was only brandy…" she told him.

"Well, take this back and go find me what I asked for" he seethed.

"I will not!" she refused, standing stubbornly. She crossed her arms.

Mac jumped up and grabbed Carman by her neck. "What da fuck did I tell you to do?"

Carman was frightened, but answered. "I won't do it" defiance in her hazel eyes. She disobeyed, breaking the rule of their agreement this weekend; for her to comply with all terms. Mac slapped her. Not hard, just hard enough to show her who was boss. He let her go and took a seat back in his leather chair.

"I don't like disobedience" he said, pulling Carman over his lap. He yanked her skirt up and pulled her thong down to her ankles. "I'm gonna teach you to be obedient" he spoke sternly bringing his open hand down on her bottom.

He was spanking her. The realization caused her pulse to quicken with a surge of excitement. Her mind flashed back to when she was in junior high and had been sent to Principal Drew's office. How she had wished he would've taken her over his lap then fucked her over his desk from behind. Laying prone over Mac's lap, the cool air caressed her bare ass. The sting was marvelous. He brought his hand down time and time again. The impact of his palm coming down on her round ass cheeks was forceful. It sounded like fireworks exploding. Carman yelped from the sting on her rear.

"Ow, oh, ow, oh…" she cried, legs kicking as they dangled in the air. The more her ass burned, the harder she squirmed. "Ow, ow, ow, ow!" Tears stung her face. Not being able to bare anymore abuse, she reached back placing her hands over her ass to block the blows.

Mac took her wrists and held them in one hand and continued his thrashing.

"Please, Mac!" she pleaded. "I'm sorry… I'm sorry!"

"You're sorry for what?" he asked.

"I'm sorry for disagreeing to our terms. I promise, I'll be a good girl."

Her ass was scarlet. It wiggled provocatively. Her pussy peeked from behind like a Georgia peach, tempting him. In compassion, he stopped his assault, and ran a finger down her slit. Still holding Carman's wrist, he hoisted her up and forced her over his large desk. Nudging her thighs apart with his knees, he unfastened his jeans. Carman pressed the side of her face down on the polished surface of the rich mahogany desk. Heat radiated from the surface of her stinging ass, and permeated to her swollen clit, intensifying the burning desire of her soaking pussy. She was so excited, pussy juice cascaded down her inner thighs.

Carman positioned himself and rubbed his hard dick up and down her wet entrance, and Carman came loudly. Lubricating himself with her flowing juices, he stuffed himself in her ass hole. He began to fuck her slow and easy. He then forced her arms behind her back and recaptured her wrists. Carman was pressed down on the cool surface of the desk. Mac let go of her to take hold of her waist. He increased his pace. Grabbing the edge of the desk, she held on for dear life, as he fucked her. "Harder... harder... Fuck me!" she begged. Mac complied, fucking her harder and faster. "Yes, like that... Fuck me! Tear that ass up!" she screamed. Mac dug his his fingernails in her soft flesh of her bent hips as he hammered into her.

"Oh yeah, I'm cuming!" she wailed. As she climaxed, her ass contracted around his dick. "Yeeessss God... It feels sooooooo gooooooood!" she shouted. Her released triggered his own. He pulled out, and his pulsing dick erupted like a geyser. His body shuddered and he grunted as he stroked the final rivulets out. His semen coated her back side, running down her ass and the crack of her pussy. She turned around and looked Mac in the eyes. *Ask me to stay and I will,* she thought once again. Her eyes were pleading without saying. Mac didn't say a word, he turned and left her in the study. A new film of tears surfaced in her eyes. They spilled down her cheeks as her heart broke.

Chapter Eight

* * * * *

Monday morning, Jerome met Mac in a neighborhood corner store after he had call to meet.

"How is Carman?" Mac asked. Jerome's eyes glared with anger. He wanted to attack Mac, but common sense forced him not to. It wasn't his fault. It was more Jerome's fault. He was the one who forced his wife into such a compromising position. "I think she still mad at me..." She hadn't mentioned anything to him since her return. Mac nodded silently and extended a yellow envelope. "Now your debt is paid in full" he told him. He returned his money and Rolex. Jerome couldn't help but felling it was no more than payment for fucking his wife. A part of him wanted to ask what he and Carman did over the weekend. Another part knew it was best not to know. Ever since she had left, he felt nothing but regret.

"We done playin' poker and done bein' friends" he told Mac. "You a snake." He didn't care if Mac was a killer or not. His life didn't mean anything anymore. What was the point of living when he gave away the best reason for living? "I can't help but think you been checkin' out my dame since you knew me. And I don't fuck with niggaz like you. You cut. You stay your distance, and I'll stay mine" he said.

Mac stared at Jerome. He contemplated trumping his ass right there at the corner store. But he went against his nature. He had gotten what he wanted. Friendship meant nothing to him.

"That's fine with me" he stated coolly and walked away. He left Jerome more hurt than angry, by the lack of empathy. When Jerome returned home, Carman wasn't there. Normally, dinner would be ready, and she'd greet him with a hug and kiss. This evening, the house was dark and silent. It felt empty, and Jerome feared things may never be the same again. Carman left no note or message indicating where she was going.

* * * * *

Outside of Mac's apartment door, Carman waited for Mac to answer, rehearsing all the things she wanted to say in her mind.

The door opened, and an elegant chocolate sister welcomed her. "Can I help you…?" she asked with a touch of attitude, as if she was annoyed by her presence. Carman pushed past her own anger rising. "Is Mac home?"

"Hold up." she walked away. Mac came to the door. "Carman what are you doin' here…" He came out into the hall, closing the door behind him. "You know you can't just be poppin' up to my crib unannounced…"

"I-I thought—" she stammered. Mac cut her off. "I know what you thought. But this ain't that. Da weekend was only to fulfill your fantasies. It was only an opportunity. I never lied or misled you. I'm sorry if you were mistaken. But we can share no emotional bond. I'm married." She tried to maintain her composure. She had too much class to be fighting over a man. "Didn't it mean anything to you?" she asked.

"Nah, it was just sex…" he said coldly with a straight face. "Carman, go home to your husband. I'm sure he waitin'" he kissed her on the forehead, then turned and walked back inside.

* * * * *

Sitting on the couch, Jerome stared aimlessly at the Paid in Full movie on TV. Ironic, due to the dilemma he was in. His thoughts about Carman stopped when his cellphone rung. It was her.

"Where are you, Carman?" He checked the time on his watch. It was just past ten o'clock.

"I'm at a bar on Water street" she told him. "I need you to come pick me up" she said, her voice slightly slurred by alcohol.

"I'll be right there" he said.

The tavern was fairly crowded for a Monday night. Jerome spotted Carman in a booth, across from an attractive mulatto woman in a black dress and high heels. Carman noticed him arriving and stood to greet him with a hug and a kiss.

"This is my friend, Eve..." she introduced them when he joined them.

Jerome really didn't care and it showed on his face. "What's up, Carman? What's goin' on?" he asked. It was not like her to drink and hang out in a strange place. Carman placed her hand on the beautiful woman's shoulder with the short bob hairstyle. "I just wanted to introduce you to my new friend... Who I plan on taking home and eat her sweet pussy..." She studied his face as she spoke. He frowned. "You can either watch or join in. I want to see you fuck her, eat her pussy, then you have to fuck me while I eat her pussy."

Jerome shook his head. *Who was this woman?* he thought.

"You got me fucked up, Carman. You are not bringing another into our bedroom."

She gave Jerome a stern gaze. "Your choice. But this is how it's going to be from now on. I need a female lover, and I don't mind sharing. I did what you expected me to do over the weekend, and it opened my eyes to a whole new world. I need someone to fulfill all my fantasies. If you won't help me, I'll find someone who will. I want our marriage to work, and I believe it can."

Carman rose and took Eve's hand. "You coming or not?" she offered, then moved to leave hand and hand with her new companion. Jerome weighed the possibility. He knew he had in Carman what most men dreamed of. He could either be the man she want him to be, or leave. Leaving wasn't an option. He loved her too much. Sliding out the vinyl seat, he followed his wife out of the tavern...

The End

Also Available by Bagz of Money Content

Live by It, Die By It (By: Ice Money)
Live By It, Die By It 2 (By: Ice Money)
Mercenary (By: Ice Money)
The Ruler of the Red Ruler (By: Kutta)
The Trenches: Murder, Money, Betrayal (By: Kutta)
Block Boyz (By: Juvi)
Team Savage (By: Ace Boogie)
Team Savage 2 (By: Ace Boogie)
Team Savage III (By: Ace Boogie)
Love Have Mercy (By: Kordarow Moore)
Rich Pride (By M.L. Moore)

Available at Bagzofmoneycontent.com and most major bookstores.